The Dessert Games

A Hunger Games Parody

by
Tom H. Richardson
tomhrichardson@hotmail.com

Ὑπό Τῷ Ἡλιῷ

HYPO TO HELIO BOOKS

Houston

This is a work of fiction. Names, characters, places, and incidents are the product of the author's imagination, and any resemblance to actual persons, living or dead, business establishments, events, or locales is entirely coincidental.

This is a parody of Suzanne Collins's *The Hunger Games*. Lawyers need to be told this; everyone else will have already figured it out. In the same vein, McDonald's hot coffee is hot.

Some dialogue of *The Hunger Games* is copied verbatim in this book, since that is the nature of parody.

Soozin's invention that he shows to Karen in Chapter 1, while it is clearly in the Rube Goldberg style, is not actually from any one Rube Goldberg cartoon.

Chapter 2 jokes about the "Slide to Unlock" patent for the Apple iPhone. This is a genuine patent, properly issued by the United States Patent and Trademark Office.

Chapter 11 talks about pies that have chloroform mixed with the pie filling, and then characters eating such pies. In the off-chance that you the reader ever get hold of some chloroform, don't try making up and eating chloroform-pies of your own.

A certain famous comedy troupe made many movies, and a certain well-known joke would have worked perfectly in several of those movies. Alas, the joke was not invented till long after that comedy troupe had quit making films. Chapter 24 corrects this mistiming (sort of).

The front-cover image was created by combining three images (by Verzh, lenm, and cteconsulting), each properly licensed from Canstockphoto.com.

The front-cover font is CCToBeContinued, which is licensed from Comic Book Fonts/Active Images.

The author wishes to thank his good friend, SFC Bruce Berg (U. S. Army, retired), for being the alpha-reader for the first draft of this book.

Contact Tom H. Richardson at: tomhrichardson AT hotmail DOT com

BISAC Subject Headings:
Fic016000—Fiction > Humorous
Fic021000—Fiction > Media Tie-in
Fic052000—Fiction > Satire
Hum007000—Humor > Forms > Parodies

HYPO TO HELIO BOOKS, 2427 Clearbrook Dr., Missouri City, TX, 77489-6061

Chapter 0
A History Of The Pie-Throwing Elimination

Panem, Colorado was founded in 1952 by Dirk Capitol, an airplane mechanic who had retired from Pan American World Airways (Pan Am). By all reports, Mr. Capitol was an excellent mechanic, but he couldn't spell worth beans.

Panem, Colorado swiftly grew, so that by 1982, it had twelve high schools. (For a while, Panem had a thirteenth high school, but *that* school is never discussed in polite society.) Because nobody could agree on what to name the high schools, they were given numbers: Public High School One, PHS Two, . . . on up through PHS Twelve. The middle schools were similarly numbered: Public Middle School 5-A and PMS 5-B fed into Public High School Five, for instance.

In 1962, the Panem school system hired a new school superintendent, Verylongnameus Ice. President Kennedy was preaching the value of physical education for schoolchildren, and Superintendent Ice took up this cause. Superintendent Ice believed that the schoolchildren of Panem should be physically fit, no excuses accepted.

So Ice believed in 1962. So he still believed during "the Pork Days" (1982), when a U.S. government paper reported that Panem, Colorado had the most-overweight children in the entire U.S.A.

Superintendent Ice responded to this report with a decree: The schools of Panem would henceforth not sell dessert as part of school lunches, nor were the schoolchildren allowed to bring desserts from home.

Needless to say, this went over like spinach-and-liver casserole (which was on every Friday's menu for lunch, in all Panem schools).

Students responded by singing a protest song in front of the superintendent's office—

Will you, will you
Eat some cake with me,
And choc'late éclairs,
Fudge brownies two or three?
Ice cream on top of pie,
How tasty would it be,
If we both pigged out
On cake, pie, and candy?

The students' protests were ignored.

Parents called for Ice's resignation. He refused to resign. The school board went behind Ice's back, and hired a replacement school superintendent, Bob Smith. Verylongnameus Ice accepted his firing graciously, even inviting Smith to his house for cold beers.

During that drinking session, Smith had a heart attack. The school board was forced to rehire Ice as superintendent.

Three more times, this happened: The school board hired a replacement school superintendent, Ice invited the man over to his house for celebratory beers, the new-hire superintendent had a heart attack, and the school board had to give Ice his job back.

After this happened four times, the school board told complaining parents, "Your child doesn't *need* home-made pie for lunch, right?"

****

But not everything went Ice's way. The school board exempted all of Panem's elementary schools from his no-desserts rule.

Superintendent Ice went before the school board and threw a fit. They told him, "You need to be flexible."

Then he said something totally unexpected: "I'm willing to let *one* middle-school or high-school student earn exemption from the dessert ban each year."

They asked him, "How will you choose that one student?"

Superintendent Ice smiled coldly. "You leave the details to me."

****

Thus in 1982, the Panem Independent School District Annual Pie-Throwing Elimination was born.

Which the students dubbed *The Dessert Games*.

Nowadays, Verylongnameus Ice is an old man with a trimmed white beard. He is still Panem's Superintendent of Schools, which means that the no-dessert ban is still in effect, and the annual Dessert Games will happen soon.

Chapter 1
My Day Started Normally

Morning, the last Saturday in June
A three-bedroom house within School Zone Twelve
Panem, Colorado
Twenty miles north of Fort Collins

My sister's reflection looked at me and asked, "Karen, was I wrong to try to rescue that kitten from that tree?" Primmy didn't say, but she clearly meant, *Because look what happened when I climbed that ladder.*

My twelve-year-old sister, Primmytwoshoes Ebergrimm, had her right arm and her left leg in a cast. The moral of this story was: If you climb a ladder to rescue a kitten, don't fall off the ladder.

Or else rescue kittens from only short trees.

My sister and I had very different attitudes toward kittens. Primmy liked to rescue kittens; I had tried to drown her kitten Pollen some years ago. But Primmy had never found out about that, so my sister still loved me. Pollen? Not so much.

Anyway, Primmy was now waiting for my answer. I shrugged and said, "At least you didn't run into a burning orphanage, like that time two years ago. You burned half your hair off then."

Primmy reached over to self-consciously stroke one of her blond braids that were hanging down her back. Or at least, she *tried to* stroke the braid. With her right arm in a cast, she couldn't reach it.

After several seconds of waving her plaster-covered right arm around without achieving her goal, Primmy said, "You know how I love yellow cake with chocolate frosting? I *really* want to win this. But this year, if I'm picked, no way can I win, and then I won't get picked again. That's the rule."

I replied, "If you say that you are unable to participate, then the Selector can ask for volunteers. The first person to touch your shoulder becomes the volunteer. If he or she wins, the rules say that the winner can sign over Dessert Privilege to another student."

Primmy rolled her eyes. "Karen, whoever wins is going to eat dessert themselves, not sign it over to me. Look at the Gluttons, *they* don't sign over Dessert Privilege."

We both giggled at that. The Gluttons were volunteers from School Zones One, Two, and Four, and the Gluttons were *fat*.

But then my face lost its smile. "Primmy, there will be many names in the Selection Bowl besides yours. This problem won't come up, so relax."

****

Then I said, "But speaking of gluttony, I want to grab something to eat before I go over to Soozin's house. He's got some invention he *has to* show me before the Selection." I rolled my eyes.

I gestured to Primmy, and she hobbled out of her bedroom as I walked beside her.

When we walked into the living room, there was Mom, sitting at the left end of the couch and staring out the window. Mom was always sitting on the couch and staring out the window; she had done that ever since Dad had died in the automobile accident.

"Hold on," I said to Primmy. A spider was using Mom's arm to anchor a cobweb with. I picked up the broom that was leaning against the wall by the couch, swept Mom off again, put the broom back, then Primmy and I resumed our trip to the kitchen.

****

A half-hour later
At Soozin Hawtbod's house

Soozin opened his front door, and grinned when he saw me on his doorstep.

"Come in, Karen, you *have to* see this! You will be so amazed!"

Soon we were down in his basement. Whatever he had invented, it filled up that basement.

As tactfully as I could, I said, "I can't tell what your invention does."

Soozin grinned again. "You watch. You'll call me a genius."

Soozin pressed "Play" on a boombox (A), which made him tap the musical beat on a spring-resistant foot pedal (B), which pulled down the handle of a bicycle-tire pump (C), which caused the steady inflation of a toy balloon (D). When the balloon burst, the *bang* startled a sleeping cat (E), which leaped up into the air, slamming its head against a fireplace bellows (F), from which came a puff of air that made the flame of a burning candle (G) momentarily burn hotter and bigger, which burned a string (H) in two . . .

The end result of all this activity was that a hemispherical wire strainer (M), with its handle sawed off, dropped six feet to a place on the concrete floor that was chalk-marked *Mouse*.

I said to Soozin, "I still don't get it."

"Duh, Karen, it's a humane mousetrap. You put cheese there, you start the music, and the mice get captured without killing them."

Hoo boy. I recalled then that Soozin's father, a dentist-inventor, had been killed when his prototype dentures-making machine had exploded. Now, it seemed, son Soozin was traveling down that same path.

Worse than that was, Soozin reminded me of the rumors about School Zone Thirteen.

****

These days, nobody from PHS Twelve travelled to School Zone Thirteen—not for an away game, and not for Speech Festival, Drama Festival, Academic Decathlon, or Science Fair. Likewise, nobody from PHS Thirteen had set foot in School Zone Twelve in a long, long time.

There were three different rumors about why School Zone Thirteen seemed to have vanished. One rumor said that vampires had come to School Zone Thirteen, after some PHS Thirteen kids had held a supposedly-fake séance. Eventually the vampires had been killed off, but not before they had killed everyone in the school zone. A second rumor said pretty much the same as the first, except that the trouble supposedly had started when a PHS Thirteen kid had created a zombie virus in biology class. No, said the third rumor, what had destroyed School Zone Thirteen was that a kid in PHS Thirteen's computer-science class had invented a new video game, and had given it to everyone in School Zone Thirteen to test. Alas, the game had been so easy and uninteresting that everyone in Thirteen had died of boredom.

All this was why Soozin inventing stuff that he was not in control of, frightened me so much. I did not want everyone in Twelve to die like kids in Thirteen had died.

Actually, there was a fourth explanation for why the rest of Panem heard nothing from School Zone Thirteen, but *this* rumor, I did not believe at all. Two girls from PHS Eight had sworn up and down to me that Thirteen was alive and intact—Thirteen had just formed its own school district.

Just how stupid do you think I am? had been my reaction. There was simply no way that Superintendent Ice would have let Thirteen leave.

****

Anyway, Soozin now was traveling down a dangerous path, and I did not want him to get hurt.

But what I said aloud was, "Your rig is too noisy. By the time the strainer lands where the cheese is, the mice will have run away."

Soozin looked his contraption over, then he sighed. "Gosh, Karen, you invent stuff all the time, and it all works, and it's all successful. Look at you, a millionaire at sixteen!"

I shrugged. "I invent stuff because I have to. Mom has held only one job since Dad died, and she got fired after two weeks. So at age eleven, I had to step up. But who's going to hire an eleven-year-old for anything?"

I didn't mention to Soozin that it took a while for the invention-royalties to roll in. There had been that *awful* day when I had been eleven years old and I had been *sure* that Primmy, Mom, and I all would soon starve to death.

Now Soozin said, "I just want to invent something good like you keep doing, so Mom doesn't have to keep working two jobs. But I'm a total flop as an inventor."

"You're not a failure. Didn't you sell one of your inventions to Acme Novelty Company?"

"Yes, I did—which reminds me. My invention is in production now, and since I as inventor get a 70 percent discount from Acme Novelty, I ordered one. I paid for them to next-day it to your house; you should get it in today's mail."

"That is sweet of you," I replied. "Remind me again what you invented."

Soozin smiled mysteriously. "Let's say that I took a classic gag gift and I improved upon it."

"Now you have me curious," I replied. Then I pulled out my smartphone and checked the time. "I have to pick up Primmy. She will *not* want to be late for her first Selection."

"You don't have to, Karen," Soozin said. "Go to the Selection, I mean. Attendance isn't *mandatory*, plus sweets rot your teeth."

I thought then, *Soozin, you truly are the son of a dentist.* But aloud I said, "That's not a plan. Primmy is eager to go. She's *going* and I'm going *with her*, end of discussion."

Soozin thrust his chest out. "Then if you're going, I'm going with both of you."

I did not try to talk him out of it. Soozin was an inept inventor, but he was also the handsomest boy at Public High School Twelve.

****

Mom spoke for the first time in almost five years: "If you want, I can drive you two to the school, since it's Primmy's first Selection."

No way, I thought—just the thought of Mom behind the wheel, in the mental state she was in, would give me nightmares for a week.

Fortunately, it had been long enough since Mom's car had been driven that it had four flat tires. I never thought that seeing flat tires would give me such a sense of relief.

Plan B: Have Soozin drive the three of us to Selection. For some reason, Soozin sighed when Mom got into his car.

Soozin, Primmy, and I (and Mom) arrived at the parking lot of PHS Twelve at ten minutes till ten. We had to check in, which involved each of us showing student IDs.

As soon as we were past Check-In, Soozin took off his sunglasses. A blond senior girl stared at him.

"Hey, Linda," Soozin said. The girl fainted.

I saw teen girls act like that all the time, whenever I went someplace public with Soozin. Probably because Soozin was the handsomest boy at PHS Twelve.

"Hey, *you!* Kantkiss Evergrim!" an angry female voice now called out. "Thanks a lot for showing up and hurting the odds for everyone else."

I looked over; it was Midget Underwater who was yelling at me.

Primmy murmured, "Why does she call you *Kantkiss?*"

I murmured back, "Because I hang out with Soozin but we don't date. *Obviously* something is wrong with me."

Soozin must have overheard me, because now he said to Midget, "Would it bother you if I started dating Karen?"

Midget stared at him. "It . . . it . . . ." Then she fainted.

I said to Soozin, "Thanks."

"For what?" Soozin asked, puzzled.

Then I heard the amplified sound of a finger tapping on a microphone, followed by Principal Underwater's voice: "Boys and girls, the Selection for contestants in this year's Pie-Throwing Elimination is about to begin."

****

The first thing that happened was that we had to watch a propaganda video that was narrated by Superintendent Ice. It claimed to explain the Pork Days and why we were having annual Dessert Games—

"Obesity, terrible obesity," Ice said. "Groaning furniture, ripped seams, a belt grown too small. This was the health crisis that rocked our city. Panem's children were *fat*; they were chubby, flabby, massive, overweight, piggish, plump, porky, portly, pudgy, roly-poly, tubby, beefy bloated *blimps*, blubbery *butterballs*, each as big as a house and as heavy as a mountain. . . ."

Soozin muttered, "I *really* hate having to watch this."

I shrugged. After I had been forced to watch *How Your Body Makes Babies* in sixth grade, *this* video was nothing.

What is a shot of fat teenagers walking down a school hallway in 1982, next to a ruthlessly frank lecture on menstruation?

". . . children looked into the eyes of their parents who had loved them, protected them, fed them—and said 'Give me seconds, give me thirds, what's for dessert?' Brother ate brother's food till *nothing* remained. Then came the school exercise program—hard-worked, muscles sored. Panem's young people emerged from the lard, and a new and slimmer generation was formed. But slimness has a cost, and in Panem schools, that cost is dessert. When the obesity was removed, we swore as a city we would never know fat children again— but we would allow one exception. And so it was decreed that, each year, the various school zones of Panem would offer up one young man and woman to pie-fight for Dessert Privilege. The lone victor, bathed in sweets, would serve as a reminder of our generosity and our flexibility. This is how we safeguard our children's future health."

****

When the video ended, Principal Underwater said, "Now here's Bimbie B—oh hello, Sumbitch, glad you could make it."

Up on stage were three chairs, one of which had been vacant up till now. But Sumbitch Evertipsy managed to stumble up the stairs to the stage.

It was rumored that Sumbitch Evertipsy slept in an alley in a cardboard box. Rumor also said that the drunk had achieved only one honor in his entire life: winning an earlier year's Dessert Games. Supposedly Sumbitch had achieved this by acting clever. I could not imagine him being clever about *anything*, except at scoring free booze.

But now, once Sumbitch was on stage, he did not take his seat. He stumbled over to Bimbie Bauble, put an arm around her shoulders, and tried to kiss her on the cheek.

Bimbie mouthed something to him—it looked like *Later*— then pushed Sumbitch away. He landed on his butt.

Nobody laughed; we all were bored stiff. Sumbitch Evertipsy acting like a drunk was old news.

As Sumbitch managed to crawl over to his chair and sit in it without falling over, Bimbie Bauble walked to the microphone.

Cheerfully she said, "Good *morning*, everyone, isn't it a *wonderful* day? I'm Bimbie Bauble, and I'm normally a secretary at the Dirk Capitol Administration Building."

I thought, *The Capitol Building hires pink-haired secretaries? Girlfriend, I hope for your sake I'm seeing a wig. That way, on evenings and weekends you can look normal.*

Bimbie was still speaking: ". . . today I'll be choosing one *lucky* girl and one *lucky* boy to be contestants in the Pie-Throwing Elimination. Maybe one of you kids here *today* will be the one to win Dessert Privilege."

Nobody replied. The last student from School Zone Twelve to win Dessert Privilege was Sumbitch Evertipsy. The odds were not in our favor.

Bimbie then extended her left hand. "Ladies first." She reached into the Girls' Selection Bowl and pulled out a slip.

Let it be me, let it be me, I thought. Soozin might be a dentist's kid, but *I* wasn't.

Principal Underwater read the slip of paper with a bar-code reader, then shook his head. Bimbie dropped the slip of paper onto the stage.

This meant that some School Zone Twelve girl had not bothered to show up for Selection today, but her name had been picked. Too bad, now she would *forever* miss out on Dessert Privilege.

Bimbie reached into the bowl again. I hoped, *Let it be me, let it be me.*

Again Bimbie withdrew a slip of paper, again Principal Underwater bar-coded it, again he shook his head, and again Bimbie let the slip of paper fall from her fingers.

The same routine happened a third time. But this time Principal Underwater nodded.

Let it be me, let it be me, let it—

Bimbie Bauble was smiling like a beauty queen. "Please come forward, Primmytwoshoes Ebergrimm."

Chapter 2
I Know That Boy!

My hand was resting on Primmy's shoulder then. I felt her stiffen.

She groaned. "This is my nightmare, come to life."

"Remember what we talked about?" I asked.

She did indeed remember. She called out, "I AM PRIMMYTWOSHOES EBERGRIMM, AND I AM UNFIT TO BE A CONTESTANT."

There was a collective gasp from every female throat. I glanced around; every girl's eyes were shining with hope.

Bimbie said, "Um, I think we need to let a volunteer run up to her—"

Fat chance of that. For an instant I lifted my hand off Primmy's shoulder, then I slammed my hand back down. I yelled, "I VOLUNTEER! I VOLUNTEER AS PIE-THROWER!"

A moment of silence passed. Then my ears were blasted by a chorus of soprano and alto voices: "*BITCH!*"

****

I yanked my purse off my shoulder and shoved it at Primmy. "Hold on to this till I get back home."

After I climbed the stairs to the stage, pink-haired Bimbie gave me a beauty-queen smile and said, "Well, bravo! *That* is the spirit of the Pie-Throwing Elimination! What is your name, dear?"

"Karen Ebergrimm."

"I bet my buttons that was your sister. Don't want her to steal all the cake and pie, do we? Come on, everybody, let's give a big round of applause to our newest contestant!"

There was complete silence. Then Midget Underwater yelled, "SHE PULLED A GLUTTON TRICK!"

After Midget yelled this, she raised both hands, palms turned away from me, and then pulled in all the fingers of each hand except for the middle finger. She was the first girl to do it, but then every other girl except Primmy copied the gesture. Even some boys joined in.

It was an old and rarely used gesture in School Zone Twelve (at least, when adults were around). It meant *Get lost*, it meant disrespect. I wanted to cry then, seeing all those kids giving *me* that gesture.

Just as my lip started trembling, I felt an arm around my shoulder. Sumbitch Evertipsy stood beside me, looking at the kids. He said, "I like her! She's got—she's got. . ."

"Language, Sumbitch," I heard Bimbie murmur.

"I forget the word"—and as pickled as Sumbitch was, I completely believed this—"but Karen has more of whatever-it-is than all of you together! But besides that—"

I'll never know what else he was going to say, because Sumbitch fell off the stage and knocked himself out.

At the edge of the crowd was an ambulance, with two bored-looking EMTs standing there. One of them rolled his eyes, put his smartphone in his pocket, and walked (not ran) toward fallen Sumbitch.

Meanwhile, Bimbie patted her pink hair and said, "What an exciting day! But more excitement to come. Now it's time to choose School Zone Twelve's boy contestant."

There was no drama with the bar code this time; the first slip of paper that Bimbie pulled from the Boys' Selection Bowl, Principal Underwater nodded at.

Bimbie read the name: "Poofa Meadowlark."

****

At once I recognized the name; I had known for five years who Poofa Meadowlark was, though he probably did not know this.

He was a muscular boy, the same sixteen as me, with curly blond hair and sky-blue eyes. Now he was trying to keep his face emotionless; but for a second, I saw him smile.

And why not? Imagine what desserts a baker's son could bring to school if only he were allowed to!

Poofa climbed the stairs to the stage, then stopped in front of me, his hand out.

As I shook his hand, I noticed that he smelled like fresh-baked bread. I also noticed that his lipstick was a very subtle shade; it almost looked natural.

Poofa murmured something to me. It sounded like *Karen, you are the only girl I have ever loved,* but I was sure I misheard him.

Then Poofa walked across the stage to stand on Bimbie's other side, and she briefly interviewed him.

Does Poofa even remember that awful day? I wondered. *Probably not.*

****

Dad had died in the auto accident when I had been eleven. Insurance had paid a little money, but soon we had been broke.

Meanwhile, Mom had not been taking Dad's death well at all. She started sitting all day on the couch, staring out the window. She neither worked nor cooked dinner for us.

I had to make dinner for Primmy and me (Mom would not eat). I got *really* tired of eating macaroni and cheese!

While I was fixing breakfast one morning, I yelled at Mom: "What don't you get a job as a store-display mannequin? You're perfectly qualified to do that!"

Mom nodded slightly, got her car keys, and drove off. Without even saying goodbye.

She got the job, working at Macy's. She sat or stood in the window five days a week, and did not move a muscle. But she got fired after two weeks, when customers complained to Macy's about "the window mannequin with the dead stare."

So it fell to me to provide for the three of us, before we all starved to death. I was eleven and Primmy was seven.

One day, I went around with a box of kittens that Primmy had rescued, trying to sell them, but nobody would buy them.

I never have figured out why. Do people hate cute kittens?

Even more frustrating, the kittens kept climbing out of the box. Chasing them was exhausting.

Eventually I wound up by the back door of Meadowlark Bakery, though I did not notice this at the time. A black kitten climbed out of the box and jumped into an open trash can. I suppose the kitten smelled food.

I was reaching into the trash can, trying to capture the kitten, when I heard a woman's voice: "You! Brat girl! Get away from our trash cans! Go steal food somewhere else."

I turned around. Waving a rolling pin at me was Mrs. Meadowlark. Standing behind her, watching me, was a blond boy, my age, whom I had seen at school. His eyes were big as saucers—though maybe that was because of the mascara he was wearing.

The good news was, Mrs. Meadowlark never hit me. The bad news was, I had to leave without getting the kitten back.

To make life worse, just as I was backing away from Mrs. Meadowlark and her rolling pin, it started to rain. Within a minute, the rain was blasting down on me.

Somehow I wound up under an apple tree that was across the street from Meadowlark's Bakery. I was weak from hunger then; I let the kitten-box drop to the ground and I collapsed to the ground next to that box.

"*RRAOW!*" The kittens did not like the hard bump they had just received. Within seconds, they climbed out of the box and scattered. I did not have the energy to chase them.

In fact, I was sure I would die under that apple tree.

That was when Poofa came out the back door of the bakery. He started to go toward the trash cans, but then he stopped and looked around.

Eleven-year-old Poofa was pushing a wheelbarrow. On the wheelbarrow was a four-tier wedding cake. That cake was almost as tall as seven-year-old Primmy.

Poofa and the wheelbarrow started to move toward me, but Poofa never once looked at me. He looked to his left, to his right, up, down—but never at me.

One detail of that day that I will always remember: The pouring rain made Poofa's mascara run.

When Poofa was one foot from me, but still not looking at me, he dumped the wedding cake out of the wheelbarrow—

Boik! Splat!

Wedding cake got into my hair; crumbly white cake and gooey white frosting covered my face and all my clothes. Cake and frosting got into my mouth, not in a way I had ever wanted. (It tasted good, though.) Frosting went up my nose!

Some of the wedding cake fell into the kittens' box—

"*MEOW!*"

A white-frosting-covered kitten climbed out of the box, glared at Poofa and me, then ran off.

The top tier of the wedding cake had landed at my feet; somehow it remained intact. I read the inscription: *Hapinness and Lung Lief Tugethir, Jhon and Mayr.*

I wondered, *Do these misspelling have anything to do with Poofa trashing such an expensive wedding cake?*

Poofa leveled the wheelbarrow, backed it up, turned it around, and pushed it toward the back door of the bakery. He never once looked at me or spoke to me.

Meanwhile, I was stuffing as much of the wedding cake as I could pack in, into the kittens' box.

After the wedding cake got dumped on me, life got better for Primmy, me, and Mom.

But not for Poofa, it seemed. The next morning at school, I passed him in the hallway. He had a black eye (which his concealer did not manage to cover up). He did not say anything to me, and I did not say anything to him.

Later that morning at recess, I saw Poofa staring at me. As soon as our eyes met, he looked away, and I looked down. My eyes then saw a dandelion, the first dandelion of spring.

That was when I got the idea of an improved dandelion-digger that I could invent. That dandelion-digger patent was the start of my becoming an inventor-millionaire.

(The Apple iPhone slide-to-unlock patent? That was mine. I "invented" it during a beer commercial, because I was bored; and I submitted the patent paperwork to the USPTO as a joke. But that one patent earned me *oodles*.)

****

I had never once thanked the kid with the cake, but I had never forgotten what he had done for me.

In my mind, there always would be a connection between Poofa Meadowlark, the life-restoring wedding cake that he had dumped on me, and the spring dandelion that had started me on the road to riches. I owed him so much, but I had never thanked him. Sometimes my conscience had bothered me about this.

And now Poofa and I were competitors; it was me or him; only one of us could win Dessert Privilege. *Bleep*.

Chapter 3
The Bus Trip And Before

The Panem ISD bus that was supposed to drive Poofa and me across town was suffering from a mechanical problem, so we were stuck in the PHS Twelve parking lot. People came over to say goodbye to Poofa and me, which usually never happened after a Selection.

****

The first people to talk to me were Mom and Primmy. Primmy was crying—

"I will be *so* disappointed if you don't win, Karen. I *need* yellow cake with chocolate frosting at lunch!"

I shrugged. "I'll certainly try, Primmy. That's why I volunteered."

Primmy grabbed my arm with her one unbroken arm. "*No!* That's not good enough, to *try*. Karen, promise me you will *win!*"

"*Bleep*, Primmy, get a life. This is nothing worth—"

"*Promise me!*"

I sighed. "Fine, Primmy, I promise I'll win."

Then I turned cold eyes to my mother. "If something should happen to me—"

Primmy interrupted: "What are you talking about? Throwing around pies isn't dangerous."

I said, "I could get an allergic reaction to a pie in the face, maybe even die. I could get hit too hard in the head with a pie pan, and start wandering around with amnesia. On soap operas, 12.7 percent of characters at any time have amnesia, so it's a real danger."

Then I turned to Mom again, and my gaze again turned cold. "*If* something should happen to me, Primmy will need consoling. She's going to need you to be a mom for her. *You get it?* You can't check out like after Dad died!"

Mom looked at me, and for the second time in nearly five years, she spoke:

"Jeez, you've turned into such a *bitch*."

****

My next visitor was a surprise: Poofa's father, Mr. Meadowlark.

He smiled as he handed me a white paper bag filled with cookies. "To remind you what you're fighting for."

I was puzzled. "I'm now in competition with your son."

He shrugged. "Bertha says we need the tax deduction."

Then he looked around, clearly checking for eavesdroppers. He said quietly, "If anything should happen to you, I'll make sure Primmy eats."

I looked at him with a raised eyebrow.

He added, "Of course then I'll have to take care of Blanche too."

Blanche was my mother's name. How did he know that?

****

Mr. Meadowlark had approached me with a smile, but Midget Underwater now strode up to me looking fit to kill.

"You cheated the rest of us girls out of Dessert Privilege!" she spit.

"No I didn't," I said. "I did exactly what Primmy wanted me to do."

Then I changed the subject: "That's a nice hippo pin you're wearing, Midget. It's cute."

Midget slapped both hands to her chest, covering the pin. "Quit staring at my pin! Though actually, it was my Aunt Maybe-Baby's pin. She and Sumbitch—"

Handsome Soozin walked up to us then. "Hey, Midget," he said.

"Oh, wow," Midget said. Then she fainted.

She must have loosened the pin when she had slapped it; because as she went down one direction, the pin fell down a different direction.

I picked the pin up and glanced at it. It was a gold pin, showing a long-eyelashes girl-hippopotamus who was wearing a ballet tutu; she was winking flirtatiously.

I decided to pin the loosened pin on Midget's blouse, but found out I couldn't. The ambulance attendants had already taken her away to revive her.

Next, I thought of sticking the pin in my pocket until I could return the pin to Midget. But as active as I was going to be soon, the pin would likely fall out of my pocket—and Midget absolutely would not believe me when I told her that.

So I went with the third option: I fastened the dancing-hippo pin to my own blouse.

Soozin looked at the pin. "*Great* choice, Karen. When Ice sees that, he will blow his stack."

I recalled then that in Panem, Colorado, the "dancing hippo" was a protest symbol.

I grinned at Soozin. "Poor Verylongnameus Ice. Sucks to be him, oh well."

Then Soozin's face got serious. "Since you're in these Dessert Games, do them right. You're clever, Karen—find an angle and outplan the other kids."

"Gee, Soozin, I figured all I needed to do was to throw pies and to dodge pies thrown at me."

"You need to become a killer, Karen. Hunting other contestants with a lemon-meringue pie is no different than hunting video-game zombies."

Soozin didn't mention that most of the time I outscored him at killing video-game zombies.

Now I said, "Fine, Soozin, I'll turn into an angle-working hunter, once the Dessert Games start. But you're taking this *way* too seriously. It's just throwing pies."

From the direction of the bus, I heard a loud, metallic *slam* noise, then Sumbitch yelled, "KAREN, POOFA, GET ON THE BUS. WE'RE RUNNING LATE."

Soozin's hands zoomed out to grab both of mine. Earnestly he said, "Karen, if something bad happens to you—"

I rolled my eyes. "*Seriously*, Soozin?"

"—there's something you need to know *now*—"

Sumbitch yelled, "KAREN. ON THE BUS. MOVE IT, DEAR HEART."

Soozin still was gripping my hands. "—something I should have told—"

By now, the bus driver was walking up to me. He wore white coveralls that said "Panem ISD" and "Crayfish" over his breast pockets. He said to me, "You're a contestant, right? Get on the bus *now*."

As I walked toward the bus, I wondered, *What was Soozin trying to tell me?*

Then I decided, *It can't have been important, or he would have told me sooner.*

Most likely, Soozin was about to share something about his basement mousetrap. But why was he acting so *dramatic* about it?

****

The bus was a Studebaker. *Didn't they quit making Studebakers before I was born?* I thought. *Gee, they really know how to make a kid feel important.*

As soon as we boarded, Sumbitch headed for the back of the bus and took a seat by the window. *Fine with me. He doesn't want to talk to me? I sure don't want to talk to him.*

On the ceiling of the bus was a bumper sticker, partially peeled off. But I could still make out "All The Way With LBJ."

Meanwhile, as soon as the bus started rolling, the driver announced, "It will take us longer than usual to get there. This bus won't go in fifth gear."

Seconds later, I heard loud mechanical noises and whining.

"Change that," the driver announced. "I can't go in fifth gear or fourth gear."

BANG. WHIIIINE. THUMP-THUMP.

He added, "Third gear's a wash too."

BANG-THUMPA-BUMPA-WHIIIINE.

I said, "Let me guess: No second gear either?"

The driver sounded impressed: "What are you, psychic?"

We wound up traveling to the school-district stadium in *first gear* the entire way, zooming at a breakneck 10 mph.

****

Poofa kept staring at me on the bus. Several times he would open his mouth to speak, but then he would shut his mouth again.

Finally he said, "You weren't wearing that pin at the Selection."

I nodded. "It's Midget's pin."

Poofa said, "Midget's the *last* person I would figure to be a troublemaker. You know what that pin means, don't you?"

I nodded. "Soozin reminded me."

For some reason, Poofa frowned and turned away.

Up close, I noticed that Poofa's foundation closely matched his skin tone. He was no newbie at wearing makeup.

With Poofa no longer talking to me, and I having no interest in talking to Sumbitch or Bimbie, I thought about the pin that I had borrowed.

At the time of the first Dessert Games, the students had resented Ice denying them dessert at school. (And they still felt that way, even now.) When it had become clear that nobody was getting cake or pie for lunch unless they played Ice's silly game, the students had passed the hat in every School Zone; the result was lots of dancing-hippo pins being made. When two kids were Selected in each School Zone, those two kids were given the pins to wear.

In the first Dessert Games, twenty-four kids had been Selected, and twenty-four kids had worn dancing-hippo pins.

Those pins had sent Ice a message: *You make me get hit in the face with pies, because I am fat and supposedly that is so terrible? If I am fat, I am proud of it!*

But that dancing-hippo-pin protest had been long ago—goodness, back in 1982. Had anyone cared when Midget's Aunt Maybe-Baby had worn the pin, years later?

Would anyone care if I wore the dancing-hippo pin *now?*

****

Soon after this, I sighed. "There's nothing to do on this bus, and it'll take us forever to get where we're going." What with our bus's 10-mph limitation, we were still pretty near to PHS Twelve.

Bimbie looked at Poofa and me and said cheerfully, "Would you like something to eat? You need to keep your energy up. I have free food for you, through the generosity of the Capitol Building."

Bimbie reached into a plastic grocery sack that I had not noticed before, and pulled out two bags of trail mix. She handed Poofa and me each a bag.

My bag was 16 ounces by weight. I guessed that it would have cost me five bucks if I had bought it myself.

I said to Bimbie, "I am overwhelmed by the 'generosity' of the Capitol Building."

"Oh, you should be! When I started doing this, each contestant was given only a little tub of mac-and-cheese."

Then Bimbie shoved her hand out in a *Stop* gesture, because Poofa was opening his bag. "Not yet, not yet! I need to hand out the silverware first."

"*Silverware?*" Poofa and I said together.

Bimbie stood up then, and walked over to the seat across the aisle from her. She picked up two breakfast trays; she handed one each to Poofa and me.

"Thank you, Bimbie," Poofa said, with me echoing those words a second later. Bimbie beamed at us.

Poofa and I shared a *Does this make sense to you?* look, then we each put our breakfast tray over our lap.

Bimbie picked up a third breakfast tray and a third bag of trail mix, which she carried to the back of the bus to Sumbitch. Sumbitch took the items without looking at her.

Then Bimbie walked back to the front of the bus and fetched honest-to-god sterling-silver flatware. As before, Poofa and I, then Sumbitch, each got a set. As before, Poofa and I thanked Bimbie, but Sumbitch did not.

As Bimbie was walking forward, after handing the silverware to Sumbitch, I heard her mutter, "He's a dear, but he's so *rude* sometimes."

"And finally," Bimbie announced, "the plates and napkins."

The plates turned out to be made of fine white china. The napkins were pink linen, each one in a wooden napkin ring.

Then Bimbie dealt herself a breakfast tray, set of flatware, china plate, napkin, and trail-mix bag. She opened the bag; but instead of reaching her hand into the bag, she poured raisins and nuts onto her plate.

She picked up a spoon. "Dig in, children!" she said brightly. "You need energy!"

Poofa and I exchanged a look, then we each reached a hand into our own bag.

"*Stop!*" Bimbie said. "Use your fork and spoon. That's what they're there for."

"Why not use our hands?" I asked.

Bimbie shuddered. "It's bad manners, young lady. Eating food with your hands is *always* bad manners."

So Poofa and I poured our trail mix onto our plates, and each of us ate it with a spoon. When Poofa used a knife and fork to cut a raisin in two, Bimbie beamed at him.

She said, "I'm so glad you're not like Twelve's contestants last year. I simply could *not* convince them to stop eating the trail mix with their hands. Such bad manners!"

Bimbie's trash-talk of School Zone Twelve kids offended me. Soon after, I maybe accidentally picked up my sterling-silver knife and maybe accidentally licked the entire blade.

Bimbie saw all this and frowned, but said nothing.

****

About then, there was noise from the back of the bus. Sumbitch suddenly stood up—

Bump-thumpa went the breakfast tray, as it hit the floor.

Cl-clang! went the silverware, as it hit the floor.

Crash! went the china plate, as it broke.

A spray of raisins and nuts flew all over the back of the bus.

—Sumbitch grabbed the latches for the top half of the window, yanked the top window down, and jammed his head out the window.

He vomited then, out the window. *Ugh*, it smelled awful!

Then Sumbitch went limp and fell backward. He landed on the floor of the back of the bus, passed out. His pink napkin fluttered down and landed on his paunch.

Poofa said nothing. Myself, I was in shock.

Bimbie *tsk*ed. "Sumbitch, you must stop doing this."

Chapter 4
A Deal With Sumbitch

Crayfish, the bus driver, stopped the bus seconds later. "One of you needs to clean him up. I'm not turning this bus back in to the bus pool with it smelling like puke."

Soon after, we stopped at a name-brand gas station, one that had a repair bay.

Bus driver Crayfish took upon himself the job of cleaning the outside of the bus. He used paper towels, water that he tossed from his coffee mug, and a squeegee.

Inside, Poofa was wiping down Sumbitch with paper towels that Poofa was throwing into a plastic bag.

Meanwhile, Bimbie fluttered and flitted, and wrung her hands: "Oh my goodness, we will be *so late!* This is ruining the schedule."

She had a point; Sumbitch needed to be cleaned up much faster. It was up to me to find a way.

The only problem: My kneeling in yuck, and getting wet and stinky yuck on my hands, was not something I wanted.

Too bad Studebaker buses don't come with their own shower that I could stick Sumbitch in, fully clothed.

That idea would not work, but it gave me an idea that *would* work—maybe.

A minute later, I was back on the bus, lugging a bucket that I had borrowed from the gas station's repair bay. In the repair bay was a deep sink, and that's where I had filled the bucket halfway up.

I carried the bucket into the bus and to the back. Then I poured water—*splash!*—on Sumbitch's face, shirt, and pants, every place I saw yuck.

Okay, maybe I poured more water on Sumbitch's face than I needed to.

Anyway, Sumbitch woke up spluttering.

Neither Sumbitch, Poofa, Bimbie, nor Crayfish thanked me, but my trick worked. Two minutes later, we were rolling; and the bus smelled merely unpleasant, not awful.

****

As soon as the bus was moving again, I muttered to the world at large, "This is sure a lot of hassle for one five-minute pie fight."

Bimbie looked horrified. "Oh no, my dear, this is a big, big, *big* day—it's so much more than a *pie fight*."

"What else *is* there? Poofa and I get off the bus; we're handed pies; we throw them at every other kid; and the last kid standing, wins."

Bimbie looked at me with pity. "You poor child, you don't get cable, do you?"

****

After I woke Sumbitch up, Poofa did not come up forward for a long while. As soon as the bus got rolling again—still at the subsonic speed of 10 mph—Poofa and Sumbitch started to talk quietly in the back. I could not make out their words, because the engine was whining so loudly.

After a while, Poofa came forward again. As soon as Poofa sat down next to me, he murmured something. I would swear that he said, "Karen, you're the only girl I've ever loved."

I was just about to ask Poofa to repeat this when Sumbitch came forward. Without asking, Sumbitch reached into Bimbie's sack and pulled out a bag of trail mix.

"You're supposed to give us advice," I said to Sumbitch.

While he was tearing open the bag of trail mix, he glanced over at me. "Embrace the inevitability of years of sugar-starved frustration, and know, in your heart, that there's *nothing* I can do to save you."

I said, "Trouble is, I don't like that advice. Got any other advice?"

"Here's some advice: Don't get hit in the face with pie."

Then he broke out into a strange laugh, "Ar-Ar-Ar-ar"—it sounded like the barking of a seal.

Sumbitch put the trail-mix bag down long enough to pull out a hip flask. He had just uncapped it when I growled, "You're the funniest wino I've ever met."

Just then, Poofa knocked the hip flask out of Sumbitch's hand.

Sumbitch punched Poofa in the face.

Frankly, I was surprised that Sumbitch's depth perception was good enough.

Meanwhile, the hip flask hit a side wall of the bus and landed on an empty seat. Booze was gurgling out of the flask and onto the seat cushion.

Bimbie gasped. "That's *antique* burlap upholstery!"

Sumbitch put the trail-mix bag down on his seat, stood up, and staggered over to where his hip flask was.

This annoyed me: Sumbitch punched a kid, he did not apologize, and the hip flask was more important to him than Poofa's face was?

I grabbed Sumbitch's trail-mix bag, I ripped it all the way open, and—just as Sumbitch put his hand on his hip flask—I threw the entire bag of nuts and raisins in his face.

"How rude!" Bimbie said. "Are you okay, Bitchy?"

Sumbitch looked at Poofa and me. "So School Zone Twelve gave me two eager kids this year, huh? Tell you what—

you don't say anything more about my drinking, and I'll stay sober enough to help you win."

I frowned. "Define 'sober *enough*.' "

Sumbitch tapped the hip flask with a finger. "No more than six bottles a day."

Poofa choked. "You call *that* 'sober enough'?"

Bimbie said, "Usually he drinks six bottles by noontime."

Sumbitch looked at Bimbie. "I've been busy today, so only five so far."

"Yeah, it's a deal," Poofa and I each told Sumbitch. Poofa sounded as unenthusiastic about this "deal" as I felt.

****

Sumbitch then said, "Now my first bit of advice: Whatever the t-shirt stylist wants to dress you in for the T-Shirt Parade, wear the shirt and smile."

I said, "I don't know anything about a T-Shirt Parade. I'm going to the school-district stadium to throw pies, avoid getting hit, then come home."

Poofa looked at me. "You don't get cable, do you?"

I figured out that I had said something stupid, and I did not like that at all. "You're trying to embarrass me."

Poofa replied, "I'm trying to *help* you, Karen."

I knew then what Poofa was trying to do: Get me to trust him and to drop my guard around him.

Not going to happen. Primmy was counting on *me* to get her that sweet, frosted cake at lunchtime—I was not going to let some boy from school distract me from my mission.

Not even if the boy was blond-haired, blue-eyed, and muscular.

I might, however, let myself check out his butt.

Chapter 5
T-Shirt Triumph

Sumbitch, Bimbie, and Poofa explained to me that what I had volunteered for was not a mere pie fight.

First to happen, all the contestants would participate in a T-Shirt Parade at the school-district stadium, in an attempt to gain sponsors. More sponsors, and more money from sponsors, meant that I would get to throw more pies.

No sponsor money at all meant that Panem ISD would give me only one pie to throw.

Anyway, after the T-Shirt Parade, each contestant would be interviewed at the school-district stadium—again, the reason was for each contestant to gain sponsors.

After the interviews, the twenty-four contestants would go to the school-district stadium's football field and form into a circle. When a whistle sounded, only then would we get to throw pies.

Whether I was given only one pie to throw, or twenty-one pies, once I was out of ammo, I was required to remain in the circle and be a target till I myself was hit in the face with pie.

This assumed that I had not already run out of clean face before I had run out of pie.

Now riding on the bus, I asked a sensible question: "What happens if I started throwing pies before the whistle? Or if I got hit with a pie but then I kept throwing pies at other kids?"

Bimbie's hands flew to her face. "That's against the rules. It's *cheating!*"

Sumbitch said, "Trust me, dear heart, you really don't want to do either of those."

****

Two days after leaving PHS Twelve, or so it seemed, our slowpoke bus drifted into Dirk Capitol Stadium.

Our bus parked in the parking lot, next to eleven other school buses. Also sharing the parking lot were various work vehicles; next to us was a white van marked "HFH Repairs."

Our bus was met by an old man with white hair and a trimmed white beard. Next to him was a middle-aged woman who was holding a silver tray that was covered with cookies.

When Bus Driver Crayfish opened the bus door, Sumbitch and Bimbie were the first out, with Poofa and me following close behind. I heard the old man say, "Mister Evertipsy, Miss Bauble, you're late."

Sumbitch jerked a thumb over his shoulder. "That's because your boy doesn't know how to keep a bus running."

Behind me, a man's voice said, "*Also* because of Mister Wino there. He puked on the bus, and we had to stop and clean everything off."

The bearded man paused a moment, then asked, "Would either of you gentlemen like a cookie?" The woman next to him held out the silver tray.

Sumbitch didn't take any cookies; in fact, he backed away from the tray. But a white-sleeved hand reached past me and took two cookies. "Thanks, sir," Crayfish said.

I felt irked that neither Bimbie, Poofa, nor I were offered cookies. I said as much.

"You're not hungry now, dear heart," Sumbitch murmured. "Trust me."

"*What?* Don't tell me what—"

The old man said, "I am remiss in my manners. Young lady, I am Verylongnameus Ice, Panem's Superintendent of Schools. This is my assistant, Rose White."

I casually crossed my arms in such a way that I could lay a hand over my dancing-hippo pin. "Pleased to meet you, I'm Karen Ebergrimm. But why—?"

"And I'm Poofa Meadowlark," Poofa added.

Several seconds were spent in handshaking and how-do-you-do's. At last I was free to ask, "So why did you offer cookies only to *the men?* That is pure—"

"Maybe the cookies are stale," Poofa said.

At that moment I felt a weight press against my back, which made me stagger. Bus Driver Crayfish slumped to the ground between Poofa and me.

Superintendent Ice did not bother to check Crayfish's pulse. Ice pulled out his smartphone, called 911, and reported that "a school-district employee has suffered a heart attack. I think he's dead."

Ice was utterly calm about a man maybe dying in front of him. I stared, openmouthed.

Soon after, Ice ended the call. As he was pocketing his smartphone, his assistant sighed. "Mister Ice, one day you are finally going to get in trouble for that."

Then Ice looked at all of us and said, "Come, please. You all have places you need to be. Miss White, stay with the body till the paramedics arrive."

I said, "Hold on! We can't just walk away and leave him here! He needs CPR from one of us. Not to mention, if the paramedics call the police, they'll want to talk to us."

Ice's gaze at me showed annoyance, but his voice was calm: "It would be a shame not to graduate with your classmates, Miss Ebergrimm, don't you agree? Please walk with us."

Then Ice looked at his assistant and said, "The young lady has a point. If any policeman comes here and is feeling curious, offer him a cookie."

****

The adults started to walk away then. When Poofa went with them, reluctantly I went too. But if Ice thought he had cowed me, I set him straight—

"Mister Ice, since 'no dessert' is your rule, so we must have this silly pie-throwing battle royale in order—"

"Don't say those words," Ice snapped.

"Huh?"

"We do not speak the words *battle royale* in Panem. It is forbidden."

"Whatever. Anyway, since 'no dessert' is your rule, so we must have this pie-throwing *extravaganza* in order that one of us can get past your rule, why doesn't the school district pay for the pies? Why must we all grovel to get sponsors?"

"Because sugar for pies is expensive?" Poofa suggested.

I glared at him.

Ice said, "Mr. Meadowlark has it. Put simply, the school district doesn't have a lot of coin. Coin spent on pies has to come from somewhere else—coin for computers, or computer software, or library books, or teachers' salaries. So we create a spectacle—*panem et circenses*, if you will—so private sponsors will put up plenty of coin."

I said, "I believe you have money for pies, but you choose not to spend it. I think your 'explanation' is a *snow job*."

Bimbie gasped. "Superintendent Ice wouldn't lie!"

Superintendent Ice, meanwhile, was glaring at me.

"Snow job? I'm not sure," Poofa said. "I don't know what to believe, about why we have to jump through these hoops."

Sumbitch said, "You get only two choices, kid: coin or snow."

****

While we had been talking, we five had been walking. From the parking lot, we walked toward, and then around, the Home seats of the school-district stadium.

With the words "It was good to meet you, Miss Ebergrimm, Mr. Meadowlark," Superintendent Ice left us.

More walking by the four of us took us toward the football field and the running track that surrounded the football field.

Now at last I could see what I had volunteered for.

****

Banners that were duct-taped to the front rails divided the Home bleachers into thirteen sections, which were labeled "1" through "12" and "Open." The Open section was largest.

I asked, "What does *Open* mean?"

Poofa said, "They're not loyal to any school zone. They'll sponsor anybody."

Sumbitch said, "Give your biggest smiles and waves to the Open folks, so they'll sponsor you instead of a Glutton."

"You should smile and wave to *everybody*," Bimbie corrected. "Anything else is rude."

But besides the Home bleachers and the banners at the front of those bleachers, I saw some things that confused me. On the other side of the football field, workmen were carrying wooden boards up into the Visitors bleachers and fastening them in place with power tools.

The boards were stacked up on a corner of the football field. I saw three men go to a stack of boards; their coveralls said "HFH Repairs" on the back. I wondered why three men were needed to carry one board. It turned out that the man with the strange haircut had no intention of carrying the board; he was apparently the boss. The hairless man grabbed one end of the board; but the curly-haired man yanked the board out of the hairless man's hands, and lifted the board up to carry it alongside his own head. The three men began walking single-file toward the Visitors bleachers, boss man—board man—bald man. Then the bald man said something in a whiny voice, though I couldn't make out the words. The boss man stopped, turned around, and started walking toward the bald man. The curly-haired man also stopped and turned around to face the bald man—in so doing, the board that he held hit the boss man upside the head. *Whap!* The boss man yelled at his board-carrying subordinate, and so the curly-haired man turned around to face his boss. *Whap!* The boss-man got hit upside the head a second time, by the other end of the board. The boss-man responded by walking up to the curly-haired man and poking him in the eyes. *Boink!* This made the curly-haired man drop the board—on the boss-man's foot.

I looked elsewhere, and saw two Port-A-Potties next to the cinder-block restrooms; workmen who were carrying tools and plumbing parts were walking in and out of those restrooms. On the football field, some workmen were laying down sod; other workmen were fertilizing the sod that had been already laid down. On the edge of the football field, right by the running track, was a four-inch-wide ditch; I guessed this was for irrigation pipe.

Are we contestants supposed to stand on the football field and throw pies at each other, when that means splattering landscape workers in the process?

Also at the edge of the football field, only inches from the running track and facing the Home bleachers, was—

"A *television?* What is that big television doing here, Sumbitch?" Bimbie asked.

The television was on wheels, and it was *huge*. It had an 80-inch diagonal screen, I was guessing.

Sumbitch said, "Queenie, I have no idea. But I'm headed to the concession stand to find out."

Bimbie crossed her arms. "Uh-huh, *and* to grab a cold beer *or twelve* while you're there, right?"

Sumbitch smirked. "You're wrong. I buy no more than three beers at a time."

"*Bitchy!* Not now, the kids need you!"

Sumbitch rolled his eyes, then looked at Poofa and me. "Kids, soon they're going to send you over to talk to your T-Shirt Designer. Whatever he wants to put you in, let him."

I said, "But what if—"

"Whatever t-shirt the designer has made for you, put it on and don't complain. Doesn't matter if the t-shirt is purple, it's too tight or too baggy, it hangs down to your knees, it's ripped, or it says 'I Heart *Twilight* and *Divergent*.' "

With that, Sumbitch went walking off toward the stadium's concession stand. Bimbie looked undecided for a second, then followed him.

****

I saw the other contestants for the first time.

It was easy to spot the Gluttons. Six overfed kids wore haughty expressions; the boys all were shaped like footballs, and the girls all were shaped like pears. The six of them together must have weighed fifteen hundred pounds.

The shortest of the three Glutton girls, who was so short of leg and so big of hip that from the waist down she looked like a garlic clove, was glaring at me. Why? I could not guess.

One of the Glutton girls, a blonde, would have been gorgeous if she'd been a Size Four. Alas for her, she was a Size Twenty-Four (if not heavier).

But I saw more contestants than only Gluttons—

A giant black boy was eyeing both Poofa and me; his face was unreadable. Next to him, a tiny black girl, who looked young enough to be in seventh grade, was smiling at me. A high-school girl with red hair also was watching me; she wore a sly smile.

The red-haired girl walked toward us. When she got close, she asked, "Are you contestants?"

I said, "We are. I'm Karen and this is Poofa. We're from PHS Twelve."

The redhead said, " 'Karen'? Poor girl, stuck with such an *ordinary* name. I'm Firefox, from PHS Five. By the way, I'm a web-surfing geek and I'm completely harmless, so you never need to worry about me."

While I was trying to make sense of that, Firefox continued, "The Gluttons over there, see the fat boy who's holding a barbecue fork like it's a spear? That's Marblecake, from PHS One. The blonde with the 'great personality,' also from PHS One, she's Glandular. The two kids from PHS Two are both crazy—avoid them. The fat blond boy is Cakedough; the short, fat brunette is Garlic—"

Which was an easy name to remember, since I had already decided she was shaped like a garlic clove.

"—and the boy and girl from PHS Four are named . . . huh, I can't remember," Firefox said. She shrugged.

Right then, I heard a man's voice come over the public-address system: "Attention, all contestants. Report to your T-Shirt Designers now."

"Took them long enough," Poofa muttered.

Firefox shrugged. "Doesn't bother me. I'm a patient sort."

****

Superintendent Ice had complained about the cost of the Dessert Games, but I discovered thirteen rented tents set on the grass north of the Home bleachers.

When Poofa and I found our way to Twelve's tent, we found a young man and young woman waiting for us.

Poofa walked up to the man, his hand out. "Hello, I'm Poofa. You're going to be my T-Shirt Designer?"

The man shook Poofa's hand, and said, "Hello, Poofa, I'm Centerd, and this is my partner, Partsane. Actually, I'm going to be *Karen's* Designer, because Karen volunteered for her sister. But I promise you, Partsane will take good care of you."

With that, Centerd led Poofa and me into the tent. A bedsheet hanging from the tent's center pole divided the middle of the tent into two. I saw a silk-screen setup and a portable table at the back of the tent. Oddly, on the portable table were neatly folded red, orange, and yellow t-shirts. Under the table was a suitcase.

Seconds later, Centerd and I were on one side of the divider-sheet, and Partsane and Poofa were on the other side.

Through the sheet, I heard Poofa say, "Your cornflower-colored top goes well with your skin color, Partsane."

****

I had figured that Centerd, the T-Shirt Designer for both Poofa and me, would look *unusual*. At the very least, I figured he'd have pink hair like Bimbie's. But his hair looked natural, his clothes were understated, and his only fashion excess was gold eyeliner—and very little of that.

Centerd walked over to the portable table and fetched a three-ring binder. He asked me before opening the binder, "What do you know about the T-Shirt Parade?"

"Nothing," I replied. "We don't take cable."

He said, "I'm supposed to design a t-shirt that uses your school-zone number, or your high-school colors, or your high-school mascot. I can put anything else I want on the t-shirt, even the name or slogan of a business. Then I and my partner Partsane dress you and your school-zone partner in my t-shirts, then you parade in front of potential sponsors."

I laughed. "So you're saying you have nothing to work with." PHS Twelve's school colors were black and charcoal gray, and our mascot was the Miners. Everything about our dull school was uninteresting.

Centerd said, "Previous T-Shirt Designers though so." He opened the three-ring binder and showed me photos of School Zone Twelve contestants, going back to 1982.

Every kid shown in a photo was wearing a black or gray t-shirt, with a miner drawn on the shirt. "I'm a great kid from Twelve" was the most inspiring caption I read.

Needless to say, none of the t-shirts that I saw made me want to buy pies for the kid who wore that shirt.

I handed the binder back to Centerd. "So you're apologizing in advance for giving me a boring t-shirt."

Centerd grinned mischievously. "Boring? My t-shirt design for you is *boring?* Quite the contrary."

Then Centerd's look turned serious. "You volunteered for this ridiculous contest not to help yourself, but to help your sister. The people who came here with credit cards and an open mind, I'm going to make them notice you, Karen. And Poofa, too. School Zone Twelve won't be ignored this year."

****

The t-shirt, when Partsane finally handed it to me to put on, was the biggest disappointment of my life.

What Partsane handed me was a tight-fitting black t-shirt, showing a miner (shown in shades of gray) holding a big chunk of coal. There was no slogan on the t-shirt, except for a large white *12*.

The only thing special about the image was that the coal was burning in full color—yellow, orange, and red flames.

"It's nice. It looks nice," I told Partsane politely. I spoke loudly so that Centerd, who was on Poofa's side of the sheet, could hear my words.

"Karen's decent," Partsane called out. Then she and Centerd switched places.

As soon as Centerd saw my face, he said, "You're disappointed."

"It's a clever design," I said. "Better than everything you showed me in the book."

"Ah, but this is not *all of* the design."

Centerd went over to the suitcase, put it on the portable table, and opened the suitcase. Centerd took out *something*, and carried it to Poofa's side of the sheet. Then Centerd returned to the suitcase, grabbed a *something* just like Poofa's, and brought it to me.

Centerd said, "I started with a man's XXL black t-shirt. I cut out most of the front, except for a yoke for the shoulders, and I cut off most of the sleeves. So I wound up with a black cape, with a hole at the top for the neck, and rings at the sides for the arms to go through. Then once I had my black t-shirt cape, I sewed stuff to it."

Now Centerd handed me the *something*. Up close, I saw that Centerd had taken yellow, orange, and red t-shirts, cut them into narrow strips, and sewed one end of each strip to the black cape to make layers of multicolored strips.

"Centerd, it's amazing," I said. Because it *was*.

Centerd laughed. "Wait till the breeze catches it."

****

The thirteenth rental tent, this one being much larger, covered the running track north of the Home bleachers. This big tent was where the contestants were to go once we had put on our t-shirts.

Poofa and I had to share a "chariot"—if I could call a thing that was built of white plastic pipe, particle board, hardware-store rubber tires, and chipped paint, by so grand a name.

I spotted Firefox; she and the boy next to her wore blue t-shirts with red text that read, "GO FIVE!" I was not impressed with Five's T-Shirt Designer.

Poofa hissed when he saw Marblecake's and Glandular's t-shirt. It read, "Centennial State Baker is Number 1!"

I said, "Those t-shirts are tacky, aren't they?"

Poofa murmured, "They're disgusting. Centennial State Baker is trying to put Meadowlark Bakery out of business. And besides, that yellow shirt clashes with Glandular's hair."

In the chariot ahead of us, the little black girl turned around and smiled at me. "Hello Twelve, I be Flew. You guys look amazing."

Introductions were made. Flew said the big black boy in the chariot next to her was Thrash, but he ignored us.

Then Flew turned to me. "You sure enough done volunteered for you younger sister?"

When I nodded, Flew said, "I like that."

****

No contestants were leaving the tent, because our chariots weren't being pulled by anything. But then white-coveralled bus drivers brought in our chariots' "horses"—huge, mixed-breed dogs.

Some dogs looked sort of like German Shepherds, some looked partly like Rottweilers, a few looked Setter-ish, but none of the dogs were purebred anything.

Each chariot got two "mutt horses." As soon as School Zone One's chariot was dogged, it left the tent—to the cheering of the crowd.

Seconds later, Two's chariot left. Unlike One, Two got no cheers when they came out. Instead, the crowd laughed when both of Two's chariot-dogs decided to stop and take a whiz, almost as soon as the chariot had cleared the tent.

Things went smoothly after that, as Three through Eleven left the tent a few seconds apart. The crowd in the Home bleachers neither laughed at the kids in these other chariots, nor cheered them—all those kids got polite applause.

At last, Twelve's chariot rolled out of the empty tent.

I heard someone call out, "*Look at them! Look at Twelve!*"

As the first sound of loud cheering hit our ears, Poofa took my hand in his. Surprised, I turned to look at his face. He smiled at me, and raised our hands above our heads.

The cheering got *loud*.

When we came in front of the bleachers, the crowd started yelling, "*Twelve! Twelve! Twelve!*"

I heard a teen boy's voice yell, "*You rock, Girl Seemingly On Fire!*"

I was puzzled by his remark, till I noticed that Poofa and I were being shown in close-up on the big TV. Our t-shirt capes were flapping around, so it looked like we had fire coming off our backs. Add to that the fact that we were grinning like fools and holding hands above our heads, and I had to admit that Poofa and I looked impressive.

From the north end of the Home bleachers to the south end of those bleachers, our two dogs pulled Poofa and me; and from the north end of the Home bleachers to the south end, the cheers for Poofa and me were deafening.

I smiled for the crowd like it were Christmas morning, and I waved my free hand till it was about to fall off my wrist.

South of the Home bleachers, there was a podium set up on the running track. That's where each chariot stopped.

Twelve's chariot wound up next to the chariot of Flew and Thrash. Flew gave Poofa and me thumbs-up and a big smile. I caught Firefox's eye; she looked thoughtful. All six of the Gluttons glared at Poofa and me; Cakedough and Garlic gave Poofa and me murderous looks.

Meanwhile, the plan was that Superintendent Ice would speak from the podium, and all we contestants would listen attentively while standing in our chariots. The problem was, both of Twelve's chariot-dogs decided to take a dump on the track during Ice's speech, to the laughter of the crowd.

Superintendent Ice did not stop speaking, but he glared at both Poofa and me.

That glare did not bother me, so long as Ice did not offer me a cookie.

****

I was puzzled by something that Ice said at the end of his speech—

"Contestants of Panem's Pie-Throwing Elimination, you see that we're performing repairs on the stadium. This will bring changes in the Elimination this year."

Chapter 6
Lavoxia Knew Me

Superintendent Ice announced next, "We will take a two-hour break, then we will begin interviews of the contestants. After another break of ten minutes, we will have the Pie-Throwing Elimination, which will be different than you expect. Your mentors are being given the details."

After this, our mutt-horses returned our chariots to the big tent. This was where Sumbitch and Bimbie collected Poofa and me.

****

While Sumbitch had been given several stapled pages, Bimbie had been given something much more interesting (at least to the men in our group): a voucher. This voucher was good for forty dollars, and would feed all four of us on the school district's dime.

Bimbie said, "How about we order delivery pizza and then eat here? My job today is to get the children to their appointments on time and to talk up sponsors, which I can do so much better if we spend the whole two hours here."

Sumbitch, Poofa, and I each told Bimbie some version of "BOR-ing!"

With delivery pizza ruled out, Bimbie then insisted on a place "with class," which apparently meant *someplace with waiters or waitresses that will serve us*. Bimbie did not budge from this demand.

This is how we soon walked into Dix's Truck Stop, on the outskirts of Panem, Colorado.

****

Dix's Truck Stop had been built when dinosaurs ruled the Earth, judging by the linoleum. This place had waitresses, but you'd need a microscope to find its "class."

Bimbie looked around and frowned.

When we walked in, the jukebox was playing a song about a "CB radio"—and the record was skipping. A woman with a faded pink uniform grabbed four menus, kicked the jukebox as she walked past it (which fixed the record-skip), and asked us, "Smoking or non-smoking?"

Sumbitch glared at her. "Smoking is bad for your health, dear heart. Nonsmoking, I insist."

I glanced at Poofa. Both of us had eyebrows up in surprise.

As soon as we were seated at our booth, the hostess said, "Your waitress is Lavoxia. She'll be right out."

As the hostess hurried away, Bimbie said, " 'Lavoxia'? You mean *two people* are named—"

Then a woman walked over to our table, wearing a clean pink uniform, which went well with her dark-red hair.

The woman could have been a model, and not only because of her enviable hair—she had a perfect oval face, high cheekbones, and porcelain skin.

I had admired and envied her beauty just as much, the other time I had seen her.

Strangely, Lavoxia our waitress now had red rubber balls glued to her fingertips, which made it hard for her to hold her writing pad and her pen.

The waitress and Bimbie stared at each other. Then Bimbie said, "Goodness, Lavoxia, what's *happened* to you?"

****

The waitress replied, "One of Ice's toadies caught me surfing the Duncan Hines website in a school Computer Lab.

You know how Ice hates dessert. So he fired me, but didn't stop there." She wiggled a finger, which had a red ball attached to the end.

Sumbitch said, "I'm surprised Ice didn't offer you cookies."

Lavoxia said, "He buys cookies at least a month old. He offered me cookies, yes, but who wants stale cookies?"

Poofa asked, "Where does he buy stale cookies from?"

"Centennial State something."

Poofa frowned. "It figures, Centennial State Baker selling stale cookies—they're an evil company."

Sumbitch asked Lavoxia, "Ice really did offer you cookies? For surfing a website he didn't like?"

"*Three times*—but ugh, *stale* cookies? That's when he whipped out the Superglue. Anyway, what can I bring you?"

Sumbitch, then Bimbie, gave their orders. Then Bimbie said, "Lavoxia, that is *terrible* what Ice did to you. *Very* rude."

"Tell me about it. I can't use a computer now, or text."

Poofa's face turned white. "You can't *text?*"

****

Poofa gave his food order, then Lavoxia turned to me. She blurted out, "I know you."

I shook my head hard, even as my face blushed hot. "No you don't!"

Bimbie looked at the two of us, then said, "Karen here is a high-school student. The idea that anyone who worked in the Capitol Building would know any students is ridiculous."

Lavoxia neither agreed nor argued. She just stood there, looking closely at my face.

Poofa snapped his fingers. "Karen, she thinks she knows you because you look like Delly Katessen. Delly works at a flea market on weekends."

I stared at Poofa for a second, wondering, *What is he doing?*

Then I realized, *He's covering for me, lord knows why.*

Aloud, I replied, "I don't think I look like Delly, but I've been told I do." *By you, Poofa, just now.*

Delly Katessen was a pudgy blonde with an ever-present smile; while I was tall, slim, black-haired, olive-skinned, and spent smiles like diamonds. We looked nothing alike, and Poofa knew it.

But when I glanced over, I saw that Sumbitch and Bimbie had relaxed.

After I had stammered out my order, Lavoxia stared into my face for one more second before hurrying away. By now, both our faces were red.

****

During the meal, Bimbie was eager to plan out our strategies for the contestant interview, and for the Dessert Games. But Sumbitch's attitude was "Gee, Queenie, let me eat in peace."

Bimbie reluctantly accepted that; but after the meal, I was informed, I *would* be taught how to "walk gracefully."

I suspected I would not like the teaching.

But eventually the time came when the plates were clear, and Bimbie and Sumbitch excused themselves. I didn't believe Bimbie when she said she needed to "powder her nose"; and I really didn't believe Sumbitch when he said he was "headed for the john." I suspected that Sumbitch's plan was to spend some alone-time with his hip flask.

Yet however it happened, Poofa and I soon were sitting alone in our booth. Poofa looked at me and said, "So, Delly Katessen. How amazing that you look just like her."

I snapped, "I said before, I don't know Lavoxia."

Poofa didn't call me a liar. Instead he said, "Karen, you're the only girl I've ever loved."

My face started burning again. I murmured, "Okay, fine, I know her. But I don't like the memory."

Still murmuring, still blushing furiously, I told Poofa how I had met Lavoxia before.

****

It had happened last year, during class-change: I had been walking the halls in front of the school offices when I had seen two adults talking to Principal Underwater.

The adults were each wearing white "Dirk Capitol Administration Building" windbreakers. One of the adults was a man with a crew cut; he looked like a former wrestling coach. The other Capitol Building visitor was a redheaded young woman. I thought at the time, *She is so beautiful, I'm sure her life is easy.*

Back then, Mr. Miller the Computer Science teacher had break during fifth period. Always for fifth period he would lock the door to the Computer Lab and take his break in the Teacher's Lounge. Soon after Soozin and I discovered this, we developed a scam where we'd ask our fifth-period teacher for a hall pass to the Library, we'd each Wite-Out and rewrite our hall pass from *Library* to *Computer Lab*, then we'd spend fifth period in the Computer Lab. Yes, the door was locked, but Soozin and I knew a few tricks.

(A question now, from Poofa: "Why not go to the library, since that's what your hall pass says, and there are computers in the library?" My answer: "Because there is so much more you can do with the Computer Lab machines. Remember the time that all the report cards had *Verylongnameus Ice is a moron* printed on the bottom? Soozin and I hacked Panem Schools' system from the Computer Lab.")

Anyway, that day Soozin and I were in the Computer Lab, playing around, when the door opened. It was the redhead in her white windbreaker. She sat down at a computer and started typing. She was bent over, trying to sit so that nobody but her could see the screen.

Naturally, I was curious. I figured she was surfing porn— which, she had to know, could be done only from Computer Lab (and then only with trickery). Nope, the redhead in the white windbreaker was looking at *cakes*—sweet-looking cakes with thick, gooey frosting.

(Comment from Poofa: "She was using Ice's computers to look at *cakes?* Whoa, she was *asking* for trouble!")

I understood then, why the redhead was acting sneaky. If someone in the Panem school system got caught surfing porn, he *maybe* could claim he was doing research for Sex-Ed class. But Ice had declared any use of school property for anything dessert-related to be *absolutely forbidden*.

Minutes later I was at the teacher's desk, stapling some pages together, when the Capitol Building man with the crew cut walked into the room.

I knew he did not see me, because his eyes went straight to the redhead. Who hadn't seen him come in, so interested was she in the web-page about a carrot cake.

I could have said something, given her some warning. Maybe she would have closed her browser in time if I had spoken up; maybe she never would have gotten into trouble.

But I did not speak up. When Crew Cut got just behind the redhead, he yelled, "Lavoxia, you're not supposed to be looking at this [stuff]!"

Then he grabbed her arm, yanked her out of her chair, and dragged her to the classroom door.

As the redhead was being dragged out by the man, she locked eyes with me. But I did not try to help her.

****

Now I murmured to Poofa, "I'm such a coward."

"No, you're not," Poofa said.

Then in a stressed voice, Poofa said, "It sounds like you and Soozin are close."

I shrugged. "We don't *date*. But I understand him better than any other girl does, and he understands me better than any other boy does."

Poofa said, trying to sound casual, "I'm surprised you don't date him. I understand that all the other girls think he's the best there is."

I made no reply.

****

I was the last to walk out of Dix's Truck Stop. Right by the door, Lavoxia was wiping down a table with a wet rag.

I looked at her and she looked at me. She said nothing.

I wanted so much to say *I'm sorry*, but I said nothing too.

Again I felt like a coward.

****

"Oh, *Bay*-bee! You're looking *good!*" the potbellied man said to me. I had to smile back at him, darn it.

"Hey, Joe," one trucker called over to another, "check this out. This girl's got *class*."

"I like class," Joe said, smiling at me.

As Bimbie had threatened, after dinner she gave me lessons on how to walk like a lady.

The fact that I had been walking just fine for the last fifteen years, did not get me out of my lessons.

Bimbie borrowed a phone book. For a half-hour, she had me walk a straight line in the truck-stop parking lot, with that phone book on my head. With me smiling the whole time.

As Sumbitch and Poofa watched me.

As truckers, both arriving and leaving, watched me.

As truckers *made comments* to me.

Somewhere inside that restaurant, I was sure that Lavoxia was grinning and gloating.

****

To get to the truck stop, Bimbie had needed to drive us in her car. To return to the school-district stadium, ditto.

After Sumbitch got into the passenger seat, and Poofa and I got into the back seat, I said to Sumbitch—

"Dinnertime is over. Runway training is over. Now it's time you tell me how to win the Dessert Games. What does your handout say?"

Chapter 7
Nothing Was Simple

I had said to Sumbitch, "...Now it's time you tell me how to win the Dessert Games. What does your handout say?"

He replied, "Dear heart, I'm not sure. All I know for sure is that the Dessert Games won't be over in one minute."

"*Huh?*" Poofa and I said together.

Sumbitch explained, "When I was a contestant, we stood in a circle on the football field, in front of the spectators. Behind each of us was a cart with one or more pies on it. When the ref blew the whistle, you started throwing your pies and trying to duck pies thrown at you. Once you got hit in the face, you were out. If you touched somebody else's cart, you were out. If you got hit in the face by a pie and you then threw a pie at someone else, he *wasn't* out."

"This is what I expected to play when I came here," I said.

"After thirty seconds, the ref would blow the whistle, and announce who was out of the Dessert Games, and why. If he said, 'Pie in the face,' there was no disgrace in that. But if the ref said, 'Violation of Rule Such-And-So,' by Monday, everyone at your school would know you'd tried to cheat."

"So that's what you meant by 'You don't want to be caught cheating,' " I said.

Sumbitch nodded. "After the kicked-out kids had left the field, and any kid who'd been illegally pieed had wiped off his face, then the ref started the Dessert Games back up again—for another thirty seconds."

"And this went on till only one kid was left," I said.

"And that kid was the *winner*," Bimbie said breathily, looking straight at Sumbitch.

Sumbitch smirked at Bimbie, then he looked at Poofa and me. "Anyway, that's how it's worked up till last year."

"But this year?" Poofa asked.

Sumbitch said, "The handout talks about something gold called the *Corny Dog*. Which is part of the *arena*."

I asked, "How big is this *arena?*"

"*Big.* At one time, it was going to be an eighteen-hole golf course, till Suzanne Plott-Davis donated the land to the school district. Lucky for Ice, he got her to sign the papers just before she died from a heart attack."

Poofa asked, "So what else does the handout say?"

"Beats me. Damned handout is confusing as hell—the only part I understand completely is *ESPN.*"

****

I said hopefully, "Then that means that everyone else will be confused too. And the Gluttons will be the first to go, because they move slow."

Poofa said, "And I *think* slow. If they change the rules on us, that puts me at the back of the pack *again.*"

I said, "What are you talking about? You're strong; I'm sure you can throw a pie twice as far as I can."

Poofa said to me, "But you're *smart*, Karen. I'm sure that as soon as you get in that 'arena,' you'll have a winning plan."

Poofa looked around at everyone. "You know what my mother said before I left? 'It looks like Twelve will have a Winner this year. She's a survivor, that girl.' *She* is."

I thought, *I don't have the faintest idea what is going to happen during the "new and improved" Dessert Games, or how to give myself an advantage. Yeah sure, I'm going to be the Winner!*

Then I thought, *Too bad I don't have a workable jetpack. Then for sure I'd have a winning plan!*

Thinking about the jetpack that I had never quite managed to invent, made me think of Soozin.

****

In some storybook that I had read as a little girl, the hero had a jetpack. He strapped it on his back, worked the controls (which looked a lot like video-game controls), and he could fly anywhere he wanted to go.

I wanted something like that. Then I found out that jetpacks were not real. Well, at age eleven, I decided to make them real. That way, I would get rich, which would certainly prevent Primmy from starving.

Soon after this, I built a jetpack, which compressed air and then shot that compressed air out the bottom.

It did *not* work. When I first tried it, the jetpack picked me up a few inches and then spun me forward. I landed right on my face—

FFFFFUTSSS! FWAP!

I made adjustments, and tried to take off again.

Again I wound up spinning forward.

FWAP!

The second time that I tried flying with my jetpack, I wound up skinning my nose on the pavement. *Ouch.*

Long story short, a week later I was walking through Home Depot, and I was feeling like one very humiliated young inventor. In Home Depot, I ran into another inventor-kid: fourteen-year-old Soozin Hawtbod.

Who was in Home Depot to buy parts for his hoped-for Automatic Komodo Dragon Feeder.

A komodo dragon is a huge lizard, about eight feet long, and with a forked tongue that is about an inch around. I didn't want to *touch* Soozin's komodo dragon, but I was curious to *see* it.

That day, I learned that shopping with handsome Soozin was a challenge—

"Ma'am? *Ma'am?* Would you scan my items, please? *Ma'am!*"

—female cashiers would stop and stare at Soozin's face, and I had to snap my fingers to get them back on task.

After Soozin and I shopped in Home Depot, my would-be jetpack and I soon wound up at Soozin's house, where his Automatic Komodo Dragon Feeder was supposed to be.

He told me, "Come on down to the basement, and show me how your jetpack is messing up."

I stared at him. "I can't fly my jetpack in your basement, I'd hit my head on the ceiling! Let's go to your backyard."

"Huh. I guess you're right," Soozin replied.

A minute later, in Soozin's backyard, Soozin was staring as I put the jetpack on my back, *then* I put on a kid-sized football helmet over my head, *then* I donned oven mitts on both of my hands.

He asked, "Aren't you overdoing the safeguards?"

I didn't answer; instead, I turned on the jetpack.

FFFFFUTSSS!

An instant later, the tips of my shoes, my mitt-covered hands, and the face-guard of my helmet. all hit the grass.

This was getting old, my own invention banana-peeling me. Even worse, *this* time my shame had an audience.

Thankfully, Soozin did not laugh. Instead, he said, "Let's go down to the basement and let me look at your plans."

Which I thought was an *excellent* idea. I really wanted to see his komodo dragon.

I looked around the basement as I distractedly handed Soozin the jetpack's notes and sketches. But for all my searching, I saw no sign of a giant lizard in the basement.

Soozin tapped my plans with a finger. "I see one problem right off: You've got the exhaust tubes on the outside of the jetpack instead of the inside, and that's increasing the torque that the jetpack applies to your body."

"What is *torque?*"

"You don't know? It's simple physics."

"Physics is high school. I'm in fifth grade; you're in eighth."

"The world doesn't care how old you are. If you don't know the right kinds of science and math, your invention won't work."

I changed the subject: "Where's the komodo dragon? I don't see it."

"I don't have one."

"*What?* How do you invent an Automatic Komodo Dragon Feeder without a komodo dragon to test it on?"

"Mom and Dad said I wouldn't be able to take care of it. But if I invent an Automatic Komodo Dragon Feeder and it works, then my folks have to get me a komodo dragon, see?"

"Soozin, trying to invent an Automatic Feeder for a certain animal, when you don't have that animal to test it on, is not practical."

Soozin froze motionless for a while, then he sighed. "You're right, it's a backward way to invent something."

And thus our strange inventor-relationship started. Soozin taught me science and math that he thought I needed, and I pointed out when he was thinking impractically.

We both became better inventors because of our partnership. Which was good for me, because my inventions were my only way to feed my family.

Months later, I finally got that jetpack where it could lift me up without flipping me over on my face. But that jetpack only worked for *me*—I couldn't make it work for Soozin. Then I hit twelve years old and started my growth spurt; by thirteen, the jetpack stopped working for me, too. Now when I was sixteen, the jetpack was collecting dust out in the garage.

****

When my memories stopped, I realized that Bimbie had stopped her car and had parked in the parking lot of a Target store that was a block from the Dirk Capitol Stadium. Bimbie, Sumbitch, and Poofa all had left the car and were talking together about fifty feet away.

That's odd, leaving me here, I thought, but I was not worried. I got out of the car and walked over to them.

When I got close, I said, "Let me guess: You're teaching *Poofa* how to walk like a runway model."

Poofa rolled his eyes. "You act like that's hard, but it's not. Unless you're in heels."

I wondered whether Poofa had personal experience with walking in heels.

Bimbie and Sumbitch exchanged a look, then Bimbie walked over to me. In the cheeriest voice possible, Bimbie said, "Karen, dear, why don't we go back to my car, then I coach you for your interview?"

I asked, puzzled, "Why not coach me *here?* Who knows, Poofa might learn something."

Sumbitch said, "Well, dear heart, I see a small problem with that plan. Poofa has asked to be coached *separately* for the interview."

I saw red. *"You're the only girl I've ever loved," he keeps telling me. That lying, deceiving rat!*

****

First Bimbie, then Sumbitch, tried to separately coach me for the interview.

It was a total waste of time. Even knowing that doing well in the interview would help me once the whistle blew, I couldn't convince my coach that I was sexy, or funny, or mysterious, or cocky.

I recalled a tall, blond actress, who had grown up in Louisville, Kentucky, who was always charming and cheerful whenever she was interviewed on TV tabloid shows. What I learned in Target's parking lot was that, while I had relatives in Louisville, I was clearly not related to that blond actress even slightly.

****

Not a moment too soon, the four of us were back in the parking lot of the school-district stadium. Soon after, Poofa and I were ordered to go back to the School Zone Twelve costume tent, where Centerd was waiting for me and where Partsane was waiting for Poofa.

As Poofa and I were walking from Bimbie's car to the tent, he tried to talk with me. I refused to speak to him.

It turned out that Poofa and I were in the tent to be each given aprons to cover our clothes with; we were supposed to wear the aprons for our interview and during the pie fight.

When I heard *apron*, I expected to be given something frilly with lots of white lace. Instead, my apron had irregular pieces of gauze sewn to it—the gauze being red, orange, and yellow in color. I looked a question at Centerd.

He said, "This is an apron seemingly on fire, to go with The Girl Seemingly On Fire."

Then Centerd did something strange.

Before the T-Shirt Parade, I had changed out of the blue top that I had worn here, into my "Girl Seemingly On Fire" black t-shirt and t-shirt cape. That blue top had Midget's gold dancing-hippo pin pinned to it. Now Centered gestured toward the pin and asked me, "May I?"

I nodded, though I had no idea what I was agreeing to.

Centerd unfastened the pin and put it in his pocket. Then he pulled my "fire apron" down around my head, tieing the apron's straps in back. Then Centerd took the gold pin from his pocket and pinned it to the front of my apron.

Centerd explained, "I want everyone to see the dancing hippo when they see *you*."

I didn't know what to say. "Wow," I said to my reflection.

Centerd then asked, "Are you ready for the interview?"

"I'm hopeless," I said in despair. "Sumbitch says I—I'm supposedly the opposite of charming."

Centerd said, "Baloney. I find you *very* charming when you talk to me."

"But I *won't* be talking to you. I'll be talking to some guy I've never met, in front of lots of people."

"I have an idea about that," Centerd replied. "You know how a catcher can send signals to the pitcher, without the batter knowing a thing?"

A minute later, Centerd and I had made a plan.

Compared to Centerd and me, Poofa and Partsane needed a few extra minutes to leave the tent: Poofa wanted Partsane to touch up his make-up for the interview.

****

One minute before the contestant interviews

Poofa's apron also had a fire-theme. I said to him, "Nice apron," then I gave him the silent treatment.

All of us twenty-four contestants were seated on a stage. We were facing two chairs.

One of the chairs held Sid Caesar Flickactor. He was smiling a car-salesman's smile as he called up Glandular—the female contestant from School Zone One—to sit in the empty chair next to him.

Glandular's hair was done up nice, and her apron was pink and frilly. She was meant to look attractive, I guessed.

But she waddled from her chair to the interview chair, and this ruined the effect she was aiming for.

Sid's first question to Glandular was, "We're here so that one Panem young person can eat more types of food. Speaking of food, what is *your* favorite food?"

Glandular said, "Dessert, or other than dessert?"

"Either."

"That's a tough question! I like chocolate cake, and cherry pie, and apple pie, and fried chicken, and baked chicken, and steak, and lobster—"

Sid laughed. "You like food, great! Now, tell us about your family."

"Hold on, I'm not through with my favorite foods! I like sushi, and nacho chips, and bacon cheeseburgers—"

"Glandular, we really need to move along now. Please tell us about your family."

"I have two younger sisters. And every day that I don't beat up one of my sisters, my mother gives me a cookie."

"Well, *that* is a unique approach to child-rearing—don't you think, audience?"

When the applause had died down, Sid asked, "So what is your strategy to win the Elimination, Glandular?"

"As soon as that gong sounds, I'm going to run to the Corny Dog as fast as I can run. Then I'm going to grab up pies and start throwing them with perfect aim. I intend to *win!*"

The School Zone One section of the bleachers cheered Glandular's statement. But I was bored, so I looked over at Sumbitch and Bimbie. Sumbitch was looking through Ice's handout, and my mentor looked furious.

****

By the time that Firefox from School Zone Five was in the hot seat, I had learned that Sid's first question was *always* "What is your favorite food?"

To which Firefox replied, "Henhouse eggs. They're the freshest."

"And how do you get eggs directly from a henhouse?"

"Sometimes my grandfather lets me guard the henhouse," Firefox replied.

A minute later, Sid asked Firefox, "So what's your strategy to win?"

Firefox replied, "I'll win by making clever plans and by deceiving the other contestants into thinking I'm harmless. Hey, I'm kidding, contestants."

****

Flew from School Zone Eleven was sweet. Thrash from School Zone Eleven acted on stage like he wanted to kill all six Gluttons, *and* kill Sid. Then Thrash left the stage and I was called up.

Sid asked, "So, Karen, what is your favorite food?"

"StarKist Tuna, straight from the can."

With that, I had answered the only question I was prepared for. When Sid asked me, "What has impressed you most about this stadium?", my mind drew a blank.

I found Centerd in the crowd. His fingertip was touching his chin; it meant *Be honest.*

I replied, "After being brought here in that ancient Studebaker bus? *Everything* here looks impressive!"

Sid laughed, and some in the crowd laughed. But I had not been trying to be funny.

Sid looked at me and said, "I'll have you know that the day the school district bought that bus, I rode it to my high-school graduation ceremony." Sid was smiling as he said that.

I laughed. "Come now, you're not that old!"

"Next to you, I am!" he replied. The crowd laughed.

Then Sid leaned forward, and his expression turned earnest. "When you came out of the tent with that 'fire cape,' my jaw dropped. What did you think of your T-shirt Design?"

I glanced at Centerd again; his fingertip was still on his chin. Again he was signaling me, *Be honest.*

I replied to Sid, "I'm really glad those weren't real flames. Because Poofa was 'on fire' too, and the chariot didn't carry a fire extinguisher for either of us."

Again the crowd laughed, which amazed me.

I looked over at Centerd and added words: "Centerd's 'fire cape' design was brilliant and daring, and I can't believe that I was the first to wear it! I felt like I was walking the red carpet at the Dorothy Chandler Pavilion."

Now Sid's face has gone from earnest to somber. "They called your sister's name at the Selection. She said she was Unfit, then you immediately volunteered in her place. Please tell us about her."

I did *not* want to tell Sid. But I told Centerd, and I let Sid listen in: "My sister's name is Primmy, she's only twelve, and she broke her arm and leg trying to rescue a kitten from a tree. I love Primmy more than anything. When I win, I'm signing over Dessert Privilege to her."

The entire stadium was silent.

That is, till the man with the funny haircut from HFH Repairs yelled at his subordinates, "WISE GUYS, EH?"

Sid ignored this and asked me, "What did Primmy say to you? After you volunteered for her?"

I had been honest up till now, and it felt wrong to start waffling. So I said, "She demanded that I win for her."

"And what did you tell her?"

I raised my hand, clenched it into a fist, and glared at the Gluttons. "I swore I would win. For Primmy."

With those words, my interview ended. Seconds later, Poofa was sitting where I had sat, facing Sid.

****

Sid asked, "So, Poofa, what is *your* favorite food?"

"StarKist Tuna, turned into tuna casserole."

Sid said, "Which makes Karen and you the StarKist-lovers of School Zone Twelve."

Poofa shrugged. "I suppose."

After that, Poofa took control of the interview. He joked about the old bus we had come here in, mentioned the old bumper sticker on the ceiling of the bus, and then shifted into "Sid, do you know how hard it is to put a bumper sticker on a kid's bike so people can read it?"

Really, Sid didn't have to do a thing except throw softballs to Poofa. Poofa made interviewing look easy.

Then Sid asked, "So Poofa, do you have a girlfriend back at PHS Twelve?"

I was too far away to see if Poofa was blushing, but from his sudden *un*confident posture, I was guessing he was embarrassed. "No, Sid, I don't have a girlfriend."

"Come now, a handsome boy like you? There must be one special girl. What's her name?"

"Well, there is *one* girl. I've had a crush on her forever. But I'm sure she didn't know I existed till the Selection."

The crowd murmured in sympathy. I wondered which girl in our school was Poofa's crush.

Sid asked, "This girl you like, does she have a boyfriend?"

"I don't know, but a lot of boys like her."

That explains it. He has a crush on a cheerleader.

Sid said, "So, here's what you do. You win this thing, you go home. She can't turn you down, especially if you share your chocolate cake with chocolate frosting."

Poofa shook his head. "Winning will only make things worse with her."

"How so?" Sid asked, looking confused.

Poofa blushed beet red. "She came here with me."

"You have a crush on Bimbie Bauble?"

"Not her—*Karen*. Karen is the only girl I've ever loved."

****

After the interviews, I knew exactly why I was angry at Poofa, but why did *Sumbitch* look angry?

He didn't leave me guessing. Waving around the handout, Sumbitch said, "We have a big problem."

I quit glaring at Poofa to ask, "What's our problem?"

Then I eyed Poofa and added, "Besides the *problem* of Poofa telling a fairy tale in his interview."

Sumbitch said, "There is nothing in the handout about the Dessert Games starting with a gong-sound. I figured that they would start with a ref's whistle—but according to the Piemakers, *when I asked them*, this year the PTE will start with a gong-sound."

"I'm lost," I said.

"Glandular knew about the gong, and there's no *legit* way she could have known. So I figure the Gluttons have been tipped off about lots of things about the new arena that you contestants aren't supposed to know yet."

"That's cheating!" Poofa said.

"It's *rude*," Bimbie said.

Chapter 8
The Last Minutes Before

I said, "We already knew that the Gluttons were rotten human beings. Now can we discuss *who else* is a rotten human being?"

I spun around to face Poofa. "You had *no right* to tell everyone you have a crush on me."

Poofa replied, "Why not? It's the truth."

Sumbitch said, "This boy just did you *a favor*, dear heart—"

I said, "A *favor?* He made me look like a silly teenage girl!"

"Newsflash: You *are* a teenage girl, and right now you're acting silly. He just turned you into a *goddess*. You will have sponsors out the wazoo, and sponsors mean pies."

Bimbie said, "You are striking, Karen, with your black hair and gray eyes. I wish you'd put on makeup and fix your hair, then you'd *be* a goddess. Remember that the most important thing a girl can ever do is be beautiful."

Centerd and Partsane had not said a word since the end of the interviews. Now Centerd looked at me. "Listen to them, Karen. Poofa helped you a lot."

Poofa looked at me. "You're the only girl I've ever loved. It doesn't bother *me* that the whole USA maybe knows now."

"*Aggh!*" was my reply.

****

Then Bimbie said, "Someone should be calling for the children soon. The Elimination starts in eight minutes."

Centerd said, "We'll leave here soon. Partsane and I will be walking you two over there, and you won't be moving fast while blindfolded."

"*Blindfolded?*" Poofa and I both said.

Centerd reached into his pocket and pulled out two black blindfolds; he handed one to Partsane. "I'm not going to argue about the blindfold, just like I didn't ask why it will be your T-Shirt Stylists walking you over there, instead of your Mentor and Selector. I *really* don't want Ice offering cookies to Partsane and me."

Bimbie nodded. "If nothing else, the cookies would be fattening."

****

Sumbitch looked expectantly at Poofa and me. "Anything else we need to talk about before you guys leave?"

I said, "So how did *you* win? You got all the other contestants drunk till they passed out?"

He smirked. "Not much to tell, dear heart. I was on the school boxing team, and I was *fast*. When you'd learned how to dodge a punch, dodging a thrown pie was easy. Soon it was down to just me and this giant girl senior from PHS One. She threw a pie at me, both my hands came up, I caught the pie by the pie-pan rim—"

"You *caught* it?" Poofa said.

"I caught it, I spun it around so the pie was facing away from me, and I shoved it back at the One girl's face, all in the time it takes you to sneeze."

"That was sneaky," Centerd said.

Sumbitch grinned. "Surprised the hell out of her and the Piemakers both. *And* Ice, let's not forget him."

I asked, "What did Ice say?"

"Said I should be disqualified, because nothing in the rules allowed what I'd done. But I argued that nothing in the rules *ruled out* what I'd done. In the end, the Head Piemaker gave me the win."

"So nyah-nyah-nyah to Superintendent Ice." Now it was I who was grinning.

Sumbitch said, "To show that there were no hard feelings, Ice offered the Head Piemaker and me each a cookie. Poor Joe, may he rest in peace."

"I saw it *all*," Bimbie said, her eyes shining. "I was twelve years old, sitting with my parents and sister in the stands. Sumbitch was so *clever* and *fast*, and he *won*."

I caught the way Bimbie was looking at Sumbitch. I said, "Get a room, you two."

Sumbitch looked at Bimbie and smirked.

****

Bimbie looked at her watch. "The children need to leave now. They can't be late."

Centerd and Partsane walked toward Poofa and me, blindfolds in hand. Before they put them on, I asked Sumbitch, "Any final advice for us?"

He shrugged. "Ask me next year. This year, everything's new to me."

Poofa said, "You have no advice at all?"

Sumbitch replied, his voice solemn, "Don't get hit in the face with pie."

Just as solemnly, Poofa and I nodded.

Then Sumbitch looked at Bimbie. "You think the concession stand is still selling beer?"

****

Being frog-marched over pavement and grass, when I could see nothing but black, was not a pleasant experience. *Better me than Primmy*, I thought.

To my right, Poofa's voice said, "Karen?"

"Hm?"

"Have you thought about what your life will be like after the Dessert Games?"

I shook my blindfolded head. "If I lose, my life goes back to what is was before. If I win, I sign over Dessert Privilege to Primmy, then my life goes back to what it was before. No big change either way."

Poofa said, "I don't want them to change me in there. Turn me into some kind of monster that I'm not."

"*Huh?* Like what?"

"What if I decide I *like* hitting kids in the face with pies? What if I start bringing pies to school—not to eat them, but to throw them at kids' faces?"

"Then, Poofa, I'll ask the principal to transfer you to School Zone Two. Kids in Twelve will be out of danger then, and the Gluttons will *love* you."

Meanwhile I was thinking, *It must be nice, this being the biggest worry in your life.*

****

A few minutes later, Poofa and I parted ways. Soon after, Centerd led blindfolded-me to my pedestal, which was about two feet wide and about six inches above the grass.

Soon after I had stepped up onto my pedestal, a man's voice said, "Hold still while I put your tracker on." I felt my right sock be pulled down, then something was wrapped around my bare right ankle.

While we all stood on our pedestals, blindfolded, a man's amplified voice spoke up:

Good afternoon, contestants. I am Barnacle Brained, Head Piemaker. This year's Pie-Throwing Elimination is brought to you by ESPN, by Centennial State Baker with bakeries throughout Colorado, and by Acme Chloroform! Here are the new rules for our Annual Pie-Throwing Elimination:

1) Stylists, keep the blindfolds on till I say to remove them. Do not speak to your contestants.

2) Contestants, when your blindfold is removed, you must stand on your pedestal till you hear a gong sound. That gong sound will come sixty seconds after your blindfold is removed.

3) If you step off your pedestal before the gong sounds, a referee will shoot you with a paintball gun and you will be out of the contest.

4) The pedestals form a circle around the Corny Dog. But you do not have to stay in that circle after the gong sounds; you may go to any part of the school district's property.

5) There are pies on a shelf atop the Corny Dog. A pie belongs to whoever has grabbed it. The previous years' rule, which forbade taking another contestant's pie, no longer is in force.

6) You put another contestant out when you hit him or her in the face with a pie. If you are hit in the face with a pie, you are out. When every contestant except one is out, this contestant is the winner.

7) Hitting another contestant anywhere other than the face does not put that contestant out.

8) Because you are free to go anywhere in a large area, it is possible that a referee will not see it when you are hit in the face with a pie. To prevent pieed contestants from not being put out and from pieing others, the pies' filling includes chloroform, to knock the pieed contestant briefly unconscious.

9) You will see cameras on red stands at various places. Figure that if you can see a camera, ESPN is filming you.

10) Silver drone helicopters will deliver sponsor gifts or replacement pies to you, as your mentor chooses.

11) You should be unable to remove your ankle tracker; but if you do, you are disqualified.

12) There is no time limit—as long as there are two or more contestants still in the Elimination, the game will continue. However, if we Piemakers get bored, we start throwing pies, and we do not care who we put out.

After reading out the rules, Brained said, "May you win, and may the ice cream in the cafeteria be ever in your flavor."

After several seconds of silence, Brained said, "Stylists, remove the blindfolds and then return to the stadium. Say nothing to your contestants."

****

As Centerd removed my blindfold, he whispered, "Surprise them. Be sneaky."

I thought, *I was just thinking the same thing.*

Chapter 9
The Horror, Splat, The Horror!

Sixty seconds to go. . .

About twenty-five yards in front of me was the Corny Dog. It was a gold-painted plywood cylinder that was about five feet high and about thirty feet long, rounded at the ends. From the left rounded-end extended the "stick" that ran parallel to the ground for another ten feet; the stick was about two feet off the ground.

The top of the Corny Dog was flattened slightly, so that it formed a shelf. On that shelf were lots of pies; together they stretched from left to right.

Laying in the grass near the Corny Dog were *things*. They were too far from me to tell what they might be.

Fifty-five seconds. . .

Near the Corny Dog was a workman and a stepladder, on top of which was a clock. The clock had a digital time-display and rotated so that I could see its face every five seconds.

Fifty-three seconds. . .

The Corny Dog and the circle of pedestals were set in a green meadow that was surrounded by trees. Mostly. To my right was a small lake, too perfectly landscaped to be natural. Behind me was a path that ran through a gap in the trees; through that gap, I saw a parking lot; beyond that parking lot, I saw bleachers of the school-district stadium.

At the edge of the meadow, where grass met trees or lake, stood the TV cameras—contraptions that looked like small, red-painted oil derricks on wheeled platforms. I did not bother to count, but it looked like there were almost as many of the ESPN cameras as there were contestants.

Between the contestants and the cameras were twelve black-and-white-striped referees. Each referee had a hand-held two-way radio attached to his belt. The referee for the School Zone Seven boy and myself had his paintball gun fit against his shoulder, though he was aiming it up instead of at either the Seven boy or me.

Thirty-eight seconds. . .

I turned my attention back to the Corny Dog and the other contestants. We all were still wearing our interview-aprons, each apron showing its wearer's school zone. Looking at the school-zone numbers, I noticed two things—

Firstly, we were all randomly scattered around the circle. Poofa, for example, was a third of the way around the circle counterclockwise from me; little Flew was three pedestals to my left; Firefox was a quarter-circle clockwise from me.

Secondly, I did not see any two kids from the same school zone standing next to each other.

Sure enough, the six Glutton kids were hither and yon, not even slightly clumped together. I was sure this would change *quickly* once the gong sounded.

Twenty-eight seconds. . .

"This crap has to stop," I muttered.

****

The four most loud-mouthed Gluttons—Glandular, Marblecake, Garlic, and Cakedough—had been talking trash as soon as the blindfolds had come off—

"You guys have *no* hope," Cakedough immediately had said. "The winner *will be* one of us."

"Even if *I* don't win," Garlic had said, "I'm gonna have fun hitting you peons with chloroform-pies and knocking you on your asses."

Glimmer had added, "None of you other kids *deserve* to win. You're not pretty enough."

Marblecake had said, "I might be oversized, but I'm *fast*. Like Cakedough says, you other kids are dead meat."

Now I glanced around. Flew, Firefox, Poofa, as well as kids whose names I did not know—everyone looked worried.

Except for Thrash—*he* was giving Cakedough a death-glare.

The two fat School Zone Four kids did not look worried; but at least they were not badmouthing the rest of us.

I did not think us non-Gluttons deserved to have our heads messed with. So I responded to the trash-talk by *laughing*. Loudly. Then I said—

"Give me a break, Gluttons. The four of you weigh half a ton, and now you're *chatterboxes* too?"

Garlic glared at me. "We can say anything we want."

"Only if you win, dear heart. And none of you look like you can move fast. Marblecake is kidding himself."

All the other contestants were smiling now, and nobody looked worried anymore.

Cakedough was looking around, so he also must have done the math. He sneered at me and said, "Fire Bitch, you just scored *eleven out of twelve* on my shit list."

I did not bother to reply. Instead, I turned my head to look at the clock.

Which showed 7 seconds left till the gong sounded.

****

Six seconds till the gong. . .

I had the beginnings of a plan. Maybe the Gluttons figured that we would all run up to the Corny Dog and give them easy targets, but I had spotted a loophole in the rules that meant I could win if I *avoided* the Corny Dog.

I had not figured out all the fine points in my plan. But I knew *exactly* what I was going to do when the gong sounded.

I made eye contact with Poofa. Once I was sure he was looking at me, I made a point of moving my eyes and head sideways, to look at the trees. Just to make my message extra clear, I mouthed the word *Trees*.

Poofa nodded. Which I took to mean that he would run for the trees too.

****

B-B-O-O-O-NGG!

I took off running. Not straight ahead, to the Corny Dog and all the pies there, but half-right, toward Poofa's pedestal.

But right after the gong, Poofa started running from his own pedestal straight for the Corny Dog. *What is he doing?*

"*Poofa!*" I yelled. He glanced in my direction, but kept running toward the Corny Dog. *What the bleep?*

Meanwhile, Flew and Firefox had come off their pedestals, but had not moved far; now they each looked confused and undecided. "Run for the trees," I yelled. "That's where I'm headed."

Each girl nodded and took off running—away from the Corny Dog.

Even as Flew and Firefox started running, I halted myself.

Standing up in the grass, almost at my feet, was a water bottle. Now I saw many individual water bottles, each about ten yards from the Corny Dog.

I realized that *if* the Dessert Games would take as long as I planned to make them last, then I *needed* that water bottle.

Stopping for a second won't hurt. I hope.

Once I was stopped and looking around, I saw other things laying in the grass. About five yards from the Corny Dog was a zip-lock plastic bag; when I walked up to it, I saw that inside the bag was a water bottle and two nutrient bars.

Only inches from the Corny Dog was a backpack.

I was rock-solid sure I wanted what was in that backpack.

I glanced around. Nobody seemed to be paying attention to me. What I also saw—

The Gluttons were throwing pies at other kids, and referees were standing apart and talking on their radios. These things I expected; what I did *not* expect to see were kids, their faces covered with pie-gunk, lying on the grass.

I was looking at the chubby Four boy when he was hit in the face with a pie. *Splat!* When the pie pan dropped away, his face was covered with white, gooey stuff. One second later, the pie that he was holding fell from his hand, his knees buckled, then he dropped to the ground.

Enough sightseeing! Hurry, grab the backpack.

No sooner did I put my hands on the straps of the backpack, but somebody yanked that backpack away. Lucky for me, I had a good grip on it.

The boy from School Zone Nine said to me, "Give it, girlie. I saw it first."

By now I was no longer bent over and was standing up, my feet braced, trying to prevent losing the backpack. But alas, he had advantages of both weight and strength on me.

Then a pie flew over my shoulder, and hit him full in the face. *Splat!*

He said, "Aw, shh—"

Then his eyes rolled up, he let go of the backpack, and he dropped to the ground.

One second, this boy was tussling with me for the backpack; the next second, he was unconscious.

Remind me later to write Acme Chloroform a thank-you letter.

But that thought was whistling past the graveyard; now I was remembering why I did *not* want to get close to the Corny Dog. I slung one strap of my new backpack over my shoulder, and was just turning to continue my run for the trees—

"Hey, Fire Bitch, where are you going?"

I recognized that voice. And sure enough, when I turned around, there stood Garlic only five yards away. As soon as I could see her face, she threw a lemon-meringue pie at me, using her left hand.

My hands came up, and I caught the pie.

Garlic gulped.

I wasn't as skilled as Sumbitch—meringue splattered on my braid.

My eyes moved slightly to the right, then I grinned. I said, "Hell yes, let's double-team Garlic!"

Garlic spun around to see who was sneaking up on her (nobody); but by the time she was facing me again, I had thrown the pie back. Her forearms made an *X* to block the pie, but it was a close race.

"You tried to trick me!" she yelled.

"I *did* trick you," I said. "But we'll have to chat later. Bye."

With that, I resumed my dash for the woods.

Behind my back, I heard Garlic's voice: "You and me, it's *personal* now, Fire Bitch!"

****

Once I was among the trees, I took the backpack off my shoulder and put it on the ground.

I unzipped the backpack. Inside I found a pair of cheap cotton garden gloves, two bottles of water, two granola bars, and a clear pouch full of leaves.

****

I put on the gloves, put the backpack back on my back, and, while wearing the gloves, climbed a tree. The tree-climbing was because I wanted a good way to see the Corny

Dog and meadow; and also, hopefully I was high enough that I didn't need to worry about getting nailed by a thrown pie.

I had been sitting in the fork of my tree for five minutes when I heard classical music coming from loudspeakers, followed by the Head Piemaker's voice—

"Attention, contestants. Thirteen of you are still in the contest, while eleven contestants have been eliminated. The eliminated contestants are. . ."

The School Zone Four boy whom I had seen be pieed was named Resshert, I learned. Nobody else from One, Two, or Four was out.

Firefox from Five still was in the contest, as were both Flew and Thrash from Eleven. And Poofa.

How did Poofa manage to not get pieed by the Gluttons? I wondered.

****

The Gluttons had disappeared.

My vantage point in the tree did not let me see the entire meadow—because the easier it would be for me to see Gluttons, the easier it would be for Gluttons to see me—but where I could see, I saw no Gluttons.

I saw one tiny seventh-grader—he was from School Zone Three, if I recalled right—carrying a pie and walking back and forth, like a sentry walking his post. I couldn't begin to guess what the boy was up to.

My puzzling over this minor mystery was interrupted by . . . *singing?*

From a short distance deeper into the forest, I heard a girl's voice—

Ninety-nine bottles of beer on the wall,
Ninety-nine bottles of beer.

Take one down, and pass it around,
Ninety-eight bottles of beer on the wall.

Ninety-eight bottles of beer on the wall,
Ninety-eight bottles of beer.
Take one down, and pass it around,
Ninety-seven bottles of beer on the wall.

I thought to myself, *Foolish, foolish, girl!*

And sure enough, soon I heard running feet, and Garlic's voice said, "Let's pie this bitch!"

Not soon after—ninety-four bottles were still on the wall—the singing stopped.

****

"Hi there. Thanks for leading us straight to you," a male voice sneered.

"You have a nice singing voice, Eight Girl," a second male voice said. That voice sounded familiar.

"Stuff it, Loverboy, before I punch you," Garlic snapped. "We're not here to pay compliments."

I wondered who in the Glutton Pack *Loverboy* was.

"Besides, the voices in my head each sing better than Eight Girl here," the first male voice said.

A girl's voice pleaded, "Oh please, *please*, can you at least give me a head start?"

"We might, if you were *pretty*," Glandular said. "But your zits have doomed you."

Splat!

"Twelve down, eleven to go, then I win!" a third male voice said.

****

Voices getting louder told me that the Gluttons were coming my way. I realized that if I climbed down from the tree now, they might see me. My only option was to stay where I was, and hope the Gluttons did not look up.

Because while I did not *think* I could be pieed from the ground while I sat in this tree, why take chances?

Then I got bad luck and good luck. The bad luck was that the Glutton Pack decided to confer right at the base of my tree. The good news was, none of them noticed me.

Marblecake and Cakedough walked up with some kind of stretcher-thing laying on both their shoulders. But it had shelves hanging down from the shoulder-poles, and those shelves held pies.

Glandular was wearing something similar: A red, box-shaped bag with a snap-down flap at the front, big enough to hold three pies, and whose straps looped around Glandular's neck and waist.

At that moment, my brain burned with covetousness: I craved Glandular's pie-carry bag. *But how do I get it away from her?*

Covetousness was followed by envy: How convenient the Piemakers had made life for the Gluttons! The Gluttons' hands were free, except when they were actually throwing pies; and after throwing two pies each, the Gluttons did not need to run back to the Corny Dog and grab more pies.

As for my new neighbors themselves, the Glutton Pack consisted of three fat girls, two fat boys, and a muscular, blond-haired boy. That last boy sure looked like—

"Poofa," Marblecake ordered, "go to the Corny Dog, grab a referee, and drag him here."

Chapter 10
I Found Hidden Pies

I was hiding in a tree. At the base of that tree, Marblecake said, "Poofa, go to the Corny Dog, grab a referee, and drag him here."

I thought, *Poofa joined the Gluttons? Why?*

Now Poofa replied, "Why me? Cakedough is the one who pieed Eight Girl."

Marblecake replied, "Because without Cakedough here, Garlic will pie you in a heartbeat—"

"Damn straight," Garlic muttered.

"—but I like you, Poofa, so I want to keep you around."

I wanted *so much* then to climb down from my tree, grab up a pie, and smash it in Poofa's face. But I knew that there was no way I could do that without being pieed myself.

So I remained in my tree, unnoticed, and I fumed.

Meanwhile, Poofa the traitor left his new friends for the Corny Dog.

Garlic said, "You guys are too easy. Why don't we pie Loverboy *now*, and get it over with?"

Cakedough nodded. "The voices in my head agree, seven to two. Let's pie Loverboy when we have a referee here to see."

"Nuh-uh," said Glandular. "Eliminate early the *one* boy who understands lipstick shades better than most girls?"

"Besides," said Marblecake, "we still need Poofa around so he can lead us to *her*."

Poofa sold me out? I wanted to scream. Even though I would be stupid to do that with the Gluttons so near.

****

"*But*," Marblecake added, "no way do we tell Poofa what Chewsmore told us, that the Piemakers stashed more pies somewhere on school-district property."

"I agree," Glandular said. "Don't say jack to the useful idiot."

Garlic said, "I'll believe all this talk about 'hidden extra pies' when I see them, but I ain't going hunting for pies. Not while we got plenty of pies at the Corny Dog."

Cakedough said, "Besides, how do we know your mentor's story is true? Maybe she's been hearing voices."

"You think *everyone* hears voices," Marblecake snapped.

Glandular said, "Chewsmore is 'friendly' with Barnacle Brained, so she finds out stuff that mentors aren't supposed to be told."

Marblecake said, "You guys *know* that, hidden pies or no hidden pies, I'm going to *win*, right?" He sounded smug.

I thought, *As soon as I get out of this tree, I'm going to track down those hidden pies.*

****

Two minutes after Poofa left, he returned with a referee at his heels (and a rolling ESPN camera following both of them). Then the Pack (except for Glandular and Four Girl) and the referee all hiked to where Eight Girl had gotten pieed.

They returned to my tree a few minutes later, and Cakedough was *not* happy: "I pieed her! My friends all saw it. What do you mean, it doesn't count?"

The referee said, "You missed her lower face, which is why she is woozy but not unconscious. The School Zone Eight female is not eliminated."

Even as Cakedough was taking a breath to reply, Poofa said, "I'll take care of her." He reached over to the pie-stretcher and grabbed a pie off the top shelf—

"Hey!" Cakedough said.

"I need to start pulling my weight," Poofa replied. "Sorry, bad choice of words."

Poofa and the referee walked back toward Eight Girl, as the ESPN camera followed.

Poofa and the referee returned a few minutes later. The referee announced, "The School Zone Eight female has been eliminated. The School Zone Two male and the School Zone Twelve male get credit for a half-pie apiece."

The referee spoke into his radio as he walked away.

Seconds later, classical music started playing over the speakers. After it stopped, Barnacle Brained announced that Mackenzie List of School Zone Eight had been pieed. Of course, the Gluttons, Poofa, and I already knew that.

"What song is that?" Four Girl asked. "That just played?"

"Oh, I'm *sure* Loverboy knows," Garlic sneered. "He's just the type to listen to hoity-toity music."

From Poofa: silence.

Four Girl asked Poofa, "*Do* you know what that song is? That announces an Elimination?"

Poofa waved a hand distractedly. "It's Pachelbel's Canon."

Poofa now had a thousand-yard stare. "I never knew—I never *suspected*—what it feels like to walk up to someone, look into their face, and then hit that face with a pie." Poofa took a shuddering breath. "It changes you. Forever."

Garlic said, "If you keep talking like that, I will *punch* you, then I will *pie* you. You hear me?"

This interesting discussion stopped when the golf cart drove by. The golf cart headed for the place where Eight Girl lay pieed and unconscious. A minute later, the golf cart reappeared, with a short-haired teen girl slumped against the golf-cart driver. The golf cart drove back toward the meadow and Corny Dog, and soon disappeared from view.

****

Garlic broke the silence: "Now that Eight Girl is out, and nobody else is stupid enough to sing loud for us, it's time to find Fire Bitch."

I held my breath. I was in real trouble if Poofa had seen where I had gone into the trees and he decided to blab.

Instead, Poofa spun around to point left, parallel with the edge of the meadow. "I saw her run into the trees on the opposite side of the Corny Dog from where her pedestal was."

"Then what are we waiting for?" Garlic said. "Let's go."

Cakedough said, "Our voices all agree: Twelve Girl is the next contestant to take down."

"Fine, but I *hate* walking," Glandular griped. "It makes me sweaty."

The Glutton Pack, with Poofa in the lead, walked off in the direction that Poofa had pointed.

Two minutes later, I was back on the ground. My objective now: to find hidden pies.

A red ESPN camera watched me climb down from the tree. How long had it been watching me? Had the camera shown me in the tree, royally peeved, while Poofa had been under the tree trying to make friends with the Gluttons?

****

Amid the trees, the maintenance shed was painted blue, and had a golf cart parked next to it. But nobody was around.

Set on the passenger seat of the golf cart was a folded-up garment that seemed to be white overalls, except that in one place, a little red heart was painted on. Laying against the white overalls was a rapier, and a wire-mesh fencer's mask lay atop the overalls.

Any other time, I would want to track down whom all that fencing equipment belonged to and I would be eager to pick his brain; but at the moment, I had other things on my mind.

The door was "locked" by means of an open padlock that was stuck into the hasp. Luck was in my favor.

Inside, on a worktable, I found seven lemon-meringue pies, two bottles of Acme Chloroform, and a turkey baster with meringue pie-filling on its tip.

I took the pies outside and deliberately dropped them face-down onto the ground.

I was just about to "relock" the door (that is, to put the open padlock back where it had been) when I thought of the bottles of chloroform. *Should I put them in my backpack?*

I decided against it. That stuff was dangerous to have around; and besides, I could not think of any way I would ever use chloroform.

When I walked away from the maintenance shed, there still were no people around, but a red ESPN camera was watching me. I pretended not to notice.

****

A half-hour later, I was thirsty, but not parched—and in any case, I had two bottles of water in my backpack. Still, I was at the point where I would have appreciated finding a drinking fountain.

I heard the gurgling of water, so I headed that way. In a clearing in the trees, I found a decorative concrete fountain, rising up from an artificial pond at the top of an artificial hill. Concrete "streams," which formed the legs of a spiral, went downhill from the "pond," and dumped water into a circular trough that was painted sky blue. In the circular trough, a sky-blue water pump presumably fed water back to the fountain.

It was a very pretty setup, and very mathematical. I thought, *Soozin would love to see this.*

A sidewalk approached the pond and fountain from the right, but there was no sidewalk near where I was. *No biggie.*

Both to more closely look at the pond and fountain, and to get some fresh water, I walked across a little red-painted bridge that crossed one of the spiral-leg "streams." The bridge was in the Japanese style, with no handrail and with a hump in the middle.

My footsteps while crossing the bridge were noisy. I did not worry about this.

Right when I got to the hump of the bridge, my left ankle got grabbed.

I looked down. A man-thing with long, uncut hair, a long, untrimmed beard, huge arms and hands that were covered with hair—Or was it fur? There sure was lots of hair on those arms—dirty and ragged fingernails, a big nose, and black and crooked teeth, was looking at me and grinning.

That grin looked greedy.

I'm looking at an actual, no-kidding troll, I realized. I said aloud, "Let go of me!"

"Give me something valuable and I will let you go, human girl."

"I don't have anything I can spare. Let me go."

"What is in your bag?"

"Nothing valuable. Nothing I can give you."

The troll's smile was evil. "Human girl, I'm sure you have *something* valuable for me. But I will start by looking in that bag you wear."

So saying, the troll *pulled* on my ankle. Since the bridge had no handrails, there was nothing for me to grab onto. I couldn't stop him from pulling me off the bridge.

And once I was off the bridge, what would happen next?

Then I remembered a martial-arts expert saying on TV, "When an opponent is holding you with his hand, he can't defend himself with that hand. *Attack.*"

So since the troll was pulling my left foot toward the edge of the bridge, I shoved off forward with my right foot, and pivoted around my left ankle.

Then I thrust my hips forward, yanked my knees apart, and let myself drop on top of the troll.

Since he had been trying hard to pull me off the bridge, he was already leaning back and was off-balance. I made things worse for him when my thighs slammed around his neck. As my body went down and away from the bridge, I forced him off his feet.

His entire body landed in the concrete stream with a loud *splash.*

Thankfully, I didn't hurt myself when I myself landed in the stream. Now I moved my legs so that I was kneeling on his chest—he was *not* going anywhere.

He managed to raise his face above the water. "You are trying to kill me, human girl!"

"Not so," I said.

I used my feet to spin me around so that I was facing his lower body, while always keeping my knees on his chest. I quickly unfastened his belt, yanked it out of his pants, and threw his belt as far as I could throw.

With the troll de-belted, I leaned uphill, so that my hand was set on the dirt bank that was closer to the fountain. Two seconds later, I was standing on that bank of the stream.

I looked down at the troll and said, "I'm trying to make your pants fall down, not kill you. *Big* difference."

He stood up then. I took a step back. But the troll was no longer threatening, because he was using both hands to hold his pants up. His clothing was wet, his hair was wet, water was dripping from his beard, and he was mortified with embarrassment—he looked ridiculous.

The troll said through gritted teeth, "You may cross my stream. Now begone."

At times, I have been called "Tactless Ebergrimm." *Ha!* I did not point out now that I had already crossed the stream, and so the troll's permission was unneeded.

I walked to the fountain, got my drink of water, and then left the clearing. But I made very sure that the second red bridge that I walked over, had no troll under it.

Just before I reached the trees, the troll called out, "You know that Ice *stole* the idea for the Dessert Games, don't you? Ice *stole* the idea from some guy in Japan."

****

As I was walking through the trees, looking for more hidden pies, I heard a trumpet fanfare, then I heard Barnacle Brained's amplified voice—

"Attention, contestants. Nobody has been pieed for at least fifteen minutes. We're bored. We warned you not to bore us, but *nooo*, you didn't listen."

Right after that, I heard strange sounds coming from in front of me. Rabbits and squirrels jumped out at me from the underbrush in front of me, then the frightened creatures ran past me.

Chapter 11
Pie-Catapults

HONKA-HONKA HONK-HONK!

What I was hearing made no sense—it sounded like lots and lots of . . . bicycle horns?

While I was trying to figure this out, I saw movement at the far ends of my peripheral vision. A referee, in front of me but far to my left, stepped out of the trees; an instant later, another referee left the trees in front of me and to my right.

Both referees were looking at me. *This can't be good.*

When two red ESPN cameras rolled out of the trees, I knew *for sure* that things could not be good.

Then the wall of firetrucks—fourteen of them, side by side—came out of the trees.

They were much smaller than real firetrucks, or otherwise each vehicle would not have been able to move between the trees. But they were red, stubby in the front, long in the back, and they had firemen manning them.

Correction: *clown* firemen. Two men were on each tiny firetruck, each man wearing a blue t-shirt, yellow-rubber pants that were held up by red suspenders, and a fireman's hat. But each "fireman" had clown-makeup on his face— snow-white face-skin, a round red nose, and eyebrows and mouth drawn in some unnatural (and *bright*) color.

As soon as the line of small firetrucks had cleared the trees, the bicycle horns had gone silent. But soon—

HONK H-HONK HONK-HONK-HONK!

The firetrucks directly in front of me resumed their racket.

While the clown at the front of each firetruck was honking his bicycle horn and driving his firetruck, the clown in back was doing . . . I couldn't tell what.

But I figured it out really fast when—

SPANG!

—suddenly I saw what looked like a giant spoon at the back of one firetruck, zoom up and forward and then instantly stop, which sent a pie flying toward me.

SPANG SP-SPANG!

Less than a second after the first pie was catapulted at me, three more pies were headed my way.

One pie hit me in the knees, one clipped my hip, one missed me altogether, and one—

—would have eliminated me if my arms hadn't protected my face.

I decided that I had spent enough time gazing at the wall of firetrucks. I turned around and did a high-speed mosey.

SPANG! SPANG!

Splat! Whoosh!

For some reason, the clown-firemen behind me were still shooting pies at me, even though when one hit me in the back, it did not count.

HONK! HONK! Those clown-firemen were making an awful racket behind me with their bicycle horns. Now I had to worry about the noise tipping-off the Gluttons: *Come over here, we've found you a contestant!*

Fortunately, before I got completely winded at running, the noise and catapult-launched pies behind me stopped.

I thought, *That was interesting, but now back to our regularly scheduled Contest. What do I do next, now that—?*

SPANG!

What the bleep? I thought. *No fair!*

This latest firetruck and two-clown crew weren't part of a platoon or company. This firetruck was a loner in the woods, and its crew catapulted a pie at me from some trees to my left.

The edge of the pie must have grazed a branch, because it tumbled end-over-end as it flew. The rim of the pie pan hit me in my upper leg. I got hit *hard*—ouch, it hurt.

I looked over at the lone-wolf firetruck. It seemed to me that the two clown-firemen's smiles weren't only painted on, they were grinning at me for real.

I stopped to look behind me (and got a pie *SPANG*'d at me for doing so). The wall of firetrucks was still coming.

HONK HONK! After the firemen behind me fired a pie at me again, their bicycle horns got noisy again.

I took off in a new direction now—or tried to. My leg hurt, which slowed me down and gave me a limp.

At one point, I stopped and looked around.

SPANG! Damn that lone-wolf firetruck, it had been matching my direction.

Whoosh—those clowns almost hit my face!

HONK HONK! Lone Wolf Firetruck's driver had to show he could be just as noisy as the other clown-firemen.

Way ahead of me and to my right, I heard bicycle horns, as other clown-firemen chased other unlucky contestants. I decided those other firetrucks were too far away to be a threat to me.

Then I heard those far-away bicycle horns honk three times slowly. It sounded like a code. Soon after, the firetrucks behind me and the lone-wolf firetruck did the same thing: *HONK . . . HONK . . . HONK.*

I watched, with mounting relief, as the wall of firetrucks, and the lone-wolf firetruck, all turned around and left me.

My relief lasted for mere seconds. Then—

Nearby, Marblecake said, "*Look* who's here!"

I hobbled to the nearest tree and climbed it as fast as I could go. I had just made my way up to the first big limb when my tree was surrounded by the Gluttons plus Poofa.

****

Everyone in the Glutton Pack was spattered with pie-gunk. Marblecake's left arm had a big bruise on it.

I noticed two ESPN cameras and a referee were watching us.

Before the Glutton Pack could say something macho, I spoke up in a cheerful voice: "Hey guys, wasn't that great, getting to see circus clowns up close?"

"Yeah, right," Garlic said, "it was peachy swell."

"Maybe we'll get to see lions and tigers next," I said, just as cheerfully. Then my voice became mock-sympathetic: "Of course, you folks at ground level would have a problem."

"So would you," Marblecake said. "Lions and tigers climb trees."

"But you Gluttons *can't*. So those big cats wouldn't have to work hard for their food."

"You're an idiot," Cakedough said. "We can climb trees as good as you."

"So you *say*, big fella," I replied. "While still standing on the ground."

Cakedough rose to the challenge. Or tried to.

I was about fifteen feet off the ground now, sitting on a limb that was as big around as my head. But to get here, I had stepped on younger, slimmer tree branches. *My* weight, those thin branches supported.

Cakedough had a hard time of it. For one thing, his feet kept wanting to slide down the bark of the tree. But after several tries, he managed to climb barely high enough that he could grab a tree branch no bigger around than a broomstick.

Then his feet slipped down the tree trunk. Cakedough briefly was hanging by one puffy hand that was gripping that slim tree branch—

SNAP!

Down Cakedough went. "*Oof!*"

"This is bull byproduct," Glandular said. "I don't need to climb a tree to eliminate you, Twelve Girl."

Glandular still had that box-shaped red bag that was strapped to her body in two places. From that bag, she now removed a pie and tried to throw it straight up at me.

Her plan failed. For one thing, Glandular's aim was off. For another thing, physics says that, for any object following a ballistic path, the higher an object goes, the slower it goes.

The bottom line: For the second time in one day, I caught a pie thrown at me. I wanted to high-five myself.

Instead, I yelled down, "Hey, Glandular, want your pie back?"

I missed, throwing the pie almost straight down, just as Glandular had missed, tossing the pie almost straight up. But if only for a second, I had a Glutton on the defensive. I considered this to be a Win, even if the referee didn't score it that way.

****

Cakedough called up to me, "Hey, Fire Bitch, you like sitting in that tree?"

I shrugged. "Beats scrubbing toilets."

"We bet you're getting thirsty. No water up there."

"Oh, didn't I mention?" I answered cheerfully. "I have two water bottles in this backpack."

"Still, sooner or later you have to come down out of that tree."

"Or you can come drag me out of this tree—silly me, that isn't an option for you guys, is it?"

Cakedough's face got red. "Just for *that*, bitch, we're waiting you out. When you come down from that tree, we'll be here—with a pie in our hand."

"*I'll* have a pie waiting too," Garlic said. "Just in case Cakedough misses."

"We *never* miss, Garlic. You know that," Cakedough said.

Garlic said, "Doesn't matter. I'm not passing up a chance to pie Fire Bitch."

"Um, I'm third with a pie," Poofa said.

"Whatever," Garlic said. "But if you try to pie one of us instead, I will hurt you."

Glandular sighed. "If the Twos are staying here, I'll stay here too."

Marblecake nodded. "I *have to* stay now—I can't carry the Pie Palanquin by myself."

Four Girl shrugged and said nothing.

Cakedough looked up and me and grinned. "Fire Bitch, we just got another idea."

****

Cakedough said, "We're going to have a party down here. We're gonna get blitzed. And even knowing that our brains are fried, you won't dare come out of that tree because we outnumber you so bad."

"How we gonna get blitzed, guy?" Marblecake asked scornfully. "Did Eight Girl share some of her ninety-nine bottles of beer with you?"

Marblecake and Glandular laughed, Four Girl smiled, and Poofa and the Twos all frowned.

Cakedough replied, "We eat some of these chloroform-laced pies, that's how. We'll get a great buzz."

"Yeah, right," said Marblecake, "and then a referee will declare us all eliminated."

"Is your head hollow?" Cakedough said. "So long as your face isn't covered with pie, the referee can't call you out even if you're passed out."

"Huh," said Glandular.

Cakedough pressed on: "You're always saying how 'special' you are, Marblecake. Wouldn't you like to get a buzz that nobody else can get? Especially if it won't cost any of us even one dime?"

Marblecake grabbed a pie, stuck in his thumb, and said, "Oh, what a good boy am I." Then he licked his thumb. "These pies have a kick, for sure."

Marblecake nodded, then looked at his blonde partner. "Glandular, you in? Poofa, you'd *better* be in."

Glandular was nodding eagerly, as Poofa said reluctantly, "Yeah, I'm in."

"*I'm* not," Four Girl said. "Have you forgotten that, not counting us six here and Nerd Boy guarding the Corny Dog, there are"—she began counting—"the redhead girl, the two kids from Eleven, the Ten boy, the Five girl, and Twelve Girl. Wait, that makes six."

Four Girl tried again: "One, two . . . two, three . . . four. No, that isn't right eith—Anyway, there are other kids out there, and *she*"—Four Girl pointed up at me—"is the only kid who we know where she is."

Garlic said, "Oh jeez, are you worried about that seventh-grader from PMS 11-C? Goodness sakes, I'm *so scared* she'll pie me."

Four Girl replied, "The *boy* from Eleven should scare you. The girl from Five is out there too, and *she* seems tricky. But go ahead, knock yourselves out."

Garlic said, "Well then, Marina, you just volunteered to stand watch while the rest of us party hardy."

"*Fine*," said Four Girl, walking over to the Pie Palanquin and picking up a pie. "I *will*." She sat down at the base of a nearby tree.

****

So five kids out of the Glutton Pack, including Poofa, began to pig out on chloroform-laced pies, while I sat up in my tree and fumed.

An hour later, I was royally miffed. When I had volunteered to take Primmy's place, I had figured that the whole shebang—the bus-ride to the school-district stadium, the pie fight, and the bus-ride home—all would take less than an hour. Instead, the way that Ice was running the Dessert Games was taking up way too much of my Saturday, and the Gluttons were wasting my time even more!

The Gluttons were right about one thing: After sitting in my tree for an hour, watching their childish "party," I was trembling. But not with *fear*.

I was glaring down at the Glutton Pack for the thousandth time when I noticed: Four Girl's "weapon" pie had slipped out of her hand.

Four Girl was slumped against her tree, eyes closed—she was asleep.

They *all* were asleep, or were passed out.

I had just decided to climb down my tree when I heard—

"Psst, Karen!"

I was in a tree, Four Girl was slumped against a second tree, and now I saw little Flew sitting in a third tree. Flew had climbed that tree to where she was as high off the ground as I was, without the Glutton Pack (or me) ever noticing.

As soon as Flew saw me looking at her, she pointed north and said quietly, "I know where more pies at."

Chapter 12
Disguised

Flew said quietly, "I know where more pies at."

I quietly replied, "Sounds great. But first I have to escape this tree without getting pied." Four Gluttons plus Poofa all were dozing directly beneath me.

Flew grinned. "*That* no problem." She was wearing a coil of rope around her shoulder; now she tied one end of that rope around the thick tree limb she was sitting on, then threw the other end of the rope to me.

It took her three tries for that rope to reach me—throwing a coil of rope is harder than it looks. But soon, I held the end of the rope in my hands.

Seconds later, I had swung down and over, and had landed gracefully on the ground under Flew's tree limb.

I did *not* scream a "Tarzan yell" as I swung on the rope. I was, after all, a mature woman of sixteen.

A minute later, Flew had untied the rope from her tree limb, re-coiled the rope and put it back on her shoulder, and had climbed down the tree.

When Flew was back on the ground, I peeked around the tree. Four Girl still was asleep, and Poofa and the rest of the Glutton Pack were still passed out.

Seeing this made me feel brave. I boldly walked straight from my hiding place to the Pie Palanquin.

After a second of hesitation, Flew followed.

Alas, my plan to pie the Glutton Pack hit a snag when I discovered that the greedy pigs had eaten three entire pies.

I needed six pies in order to pie the Glutton Pack; only five pies were left.

I whispered to Flew, "Where are those other pies you saw?"

****

Flew and I took a short walk north to a second Panem ISD maintenance shed. This one was painted red, and it indeed had pies.

The new maintenance shed also had a shopping cart; a light-green "Panem ISD" ballcap; and cans of Acme water-soluble white paint, along with one-inch brushes.

Then I got an idea. I took off my backpack and apron, and laid them on a worktable. I took off my black "Miners" t-shirt, turned the shirt inside-out, and put the black t-shirt back on. I tucked my braid down the back of my shirt. Next, I used a screwdriver to open one can of water-soluble white paint.

Flew watched all this with a puzzled expression.

I said, "Don't you think it's time the Gluttons got back what they've been handing out?"

Flew grinned.

****

I pushed the shopping cart along the ground, back toward where I had left the Glutton Pack. When I got close, I saw they all were still asleep. *My plan will work!*

Or maybe not. Up walked a referee, a real one, and eyed me up and down.

Maybe the fact that I myself looked like a referee explained his looking me over.

The real referees all wore white ballcaps; I had taken the "Panem ISD" ballcap and had painted it white. The real referees wore shirts with black-and-white vertical stripes; I wore a black shirt with white stripes painted on. On the left breast, where real referees had their names printed on, I had written "TJ." The real referees did not wear an ankle tracker; I hoped that the Gluttons would not notice mine.

The real referee looked at me, the fake referee. He thought about what he was seeing, while I hoped that he would not stop my scheme before it started.

The referee looked down at my ankle tracker, looked up into my eyes, and nodded. He made a *Get going* gesture with one hand.

I got going.

When I got near Four Girl, her eyes opened up, she gave me a sleepy smile, then she closed her eyes again.

She doesn't suspect a thing! This will be so easy.

I reached into the shopping cart. I pulled out two pies. I turned and walked toward Four Girl. I—

—then tripped over a tree root and fell down. Long story short: Both pies hit the ground, then my chin and mouth hit one pie. I was lucky: My eyes missed the pie completely.

Landing lower-face-down in the pie-pan made me gasp. I took in a mouthful of pie. My instinct was to swallow it.

As I stood up, and began to wipe pie-gunk off my lower face, I started to feel woozy.

****

I heard a giggle. "Referees aren't supposed to get pieed," Four Girl said.

I finished wiping pie-gunk off my face. Then I picked up both pies, and resumed walking toward Four Girl.

As I got close to her, I said, "Hey, what's up?"

She put a finger to her lips. "Be very, very quiet. We've got Twelve Girl stuck up in that tree there."

I looked up. "I don't see anyone. You sure it's the right tree?"

"*What?* Where'd she—?"

Four Girl did not see my right hand move. *Splat!*

After that, I ran straight for the unconscious Glandular and her pie-carry bag that I wanted so fiercely—

—or rather, I *tried to* run. I was really starting to feel dizzy now, so I wobbled on my feet.

Still, I managed—*splat!*—to pie Glandular.

Quickly I unsnapped the buckle for each of the two straps of Glandular's pie bag, yanked the pie bag away from Glandular's limp body, and ran off.

"*Hey*," Cakedough yelled, "Glandular just got pieed by a referee! What the hell?"

Marblecake said, "She's no referee, she's wearing an ankle tracker!"

Meanwhile, I staggered back toward the shopping cart.

In so doing, I bumped into the Pie Palanquin and knocked it over. *Bleep*, I had intended to throw those pies.

Anyway, once I was back at the shopping cart, I dropped my pie-carry bag on the ground; then I started grabbing pies out of the cart and throwing them like a maniac.

But I was woozy and I was in a hurry, so nobody else was eliminated.

I had presumed that knocking over the Pie Palanquin had ruined its five pies. But Cakedough walked over to it, squatted down, and stood up with a pie that did not look disgusting.

That is when Poofa ran between Cakedough and me. "Karen, get out of here! Get going! I'll hold him off."

That is exactly what I did: I grabbed the pie bag in my arms and staggered away. As I did, I heard Cakedough yell, "You two-faced, love-whipped *traitor!*"

Not long after that, somehow I was lying on my stomach, with my right cheek pressed down against the red plastic of the pie bag. Not long after *that*, the world faded away—

—to the pleasant strains of "Pachelbel's Canon." I *think* I heard Barnacle Brained announce that Glandular Smith of One and Marina Buckner of Four had been eliminated.

Chapter 13
Flew, My Friend

When I regained consciousness, I was lying on the grass by a red Panem Independent School District maintenance shed. I was confused.

The biggest thing to confuse me: Poofa had tried to save me from a furious Cakedough—real or not real?

I had never read anything about chloroform causing hallucinations—though admittedly I was no expert on this chemical—but what I remembered made no sense.

Why would Poofa buddy up to the Gluttons, then turn all white-knight when Cakedough wanted to pie me? Was that not what Poofa *wanted*, to see me get pieed?

But if indeed Poofa did stop Cakedough from eliminating me, then this was another debt I owed to the kid with the cake. I was not sure how I felt about that.

I wondered if Soozin was watching the Dessert Games on cable, then I wondered what he had thought of my disguised-as-a-referee stunt. But *that* made me recall Poofa yelling, "Karen, get out of here! I'll hold him off."

My brain did not want to think about both Soozin and Poofa at the same time; my brain got confused. I decided to think about Soozin later, on the bus-trip home.

I sat up—and realized that I was in a strange situation. My hard-won pie-carry bag, which my face had been lying on, now set on the grass nearby, next to my backpack. My balled-up apron lay atop my pie-carry bag. I very clearly remembered leaving my backpack and apron behind, inside a maintenance shed. *Was it this maintenance shed?*

Next, I realized that my black "Miners/Twelve" t-shirt was wet—and that I was wearing it right-side-out.

I checked the inside of the t-shirt, as much as public modesty permitted. The white painted stripes were gone.

How had all this happened? Did Poofa bring me here and clean me up? Was it the troll? A referee?

I could not begin to guess, though I could probably rule out the troll.

I mentally shrugged, and investigated my new prize. The pie-carry bag had white-plastic shelves to hold three pies. One of the three shelves was empty.

But the pie-carry bag held more than two lemon-meringue pies. To my delight, three granola bars were in that bag, and I was hungry!

"*Mmm*," I said, as I tore open the wrapper of the first granola bar.

Just beyond the maintenance shed, I heard a twig *snap*.

I was in the process of reacting then, preparing to go into pie-throwing battle, when my eyes saw something—

Sticking out just beyond the corner of the maintenance shed, at ground level, was a small girl's shoe. It was the shoe of a twelve-year-old girl, I recognized.

I called out, "Hey Flew, are you hungry? I've got a spare granola bar that you can eat, and I have another granola bar we can split. By the way, let's be allies."

Flew's face peeked around the corner of the maintenance shed. "You want to share you candy bars with me?"

****

Minutes later, Flew was saying, "I *love* chocolate frosting, just like you sister! Actually, I love chocolate *everything*. Chocolate cake with chocolate frosting, *mmm*."

I replied, "Chocolate-covered strawberries are nice. Ever tried 'em?"

"*No!* But now I gonna do it, soon as I get home. And soon as I talk my mama into buying strawberries for me and my sisters. What else you like, besides dessert?"

I said, "Have you ever eaten lamb stew, with dried plums in it? I've had it only once, but it's, oh my god, *delicious.*"

Flew laughed. "Maybe them plums, they come from my grandma back yard! That's how I learn to climb trees, fetching plums for my grandma. I ain't never done eat lamb stew, but I *love* turkey."

I nodded. "Turkey is good, and fresh-caught turkey is *really* good. I know somebody who hunts wild turkey."

Then I leaned close and added, "I don't mean my mentor, Sumbitch Evertipsy. He doesn't *hunt* wild turkey, he *drinks* Wild Turkey."

Flew and I became close friends fast, because we both loved food. Except for spinach-and-liver casserole, which was served on Fridays in all Panem schools.

It also turned out that Flew loved cats. I did not mention that once I had tried to drown Primmy's kitten, Pollen.

Changing the subject, I asked Flew, "How did I get here by the maintenance shed? Why didn't the Gluttons pie me while I was out?"

She said, "The Gluttons, they had to go back to the Corny Dog for more pies. By the time they come back, I drag you here, which they don't know nothing about."

"*You* dragged me here? How? Why?"

Flew grinned. "How? I be only twelve, but I know tricks. You ask me *why?* Because you be nice."

A minute later, Flew shocked me. She tapped my gold pin of the lady hippo who was wearing a tutu; Flew said, "I love to watch ballerinas. You hippo, she a ballerina. When I see this pin on you at the Parade, I know I can trust you."

✳✳✳✳

Flew and I discovered that we both loved to sing. So I suggested that we sing something together, as soprano (Flew) and mezzo-soprano (me).

We were talking over whether to sing "America The Beautiful" or "Swing Low, Sweet Chariot," when a red ESPN camera rolled into view.

I was still annoyed about Superintendent Ice changing the Dessert Games so that they were taking up my entire Saturday. Maybe Flew was annoyed too. Because when I suggested a third song, Flew agreed instantly.

So, with the nation maybe hearing every word, Flew and I smiled as we sang a certain protest song—

Will you, will you
Eat some cake with me,
And choc'late éclairs,
Fudge brownies two or three?
Ice cream on top of pie,
How tasty would it be,
If we both pigged out
On cake, pie, and candy?

****

It was Flew's idea to open our two backpacks and see what we had together. Her backpack had come with a zip-lock bag, which she had filled with berries. I had never even noticed that this place *had* berries.

Besides the bag of berries, Flew had a can of cocktail wieners and a police whistle.

When she was looking over my stuff, she picked up the clear-plastic pouch. "What this?"

"A clear pouch full of leaves?" I replied.

"Okay if I—?"

When I nodded, Flew unsnapped the flap.

She sniffed, then said, "Them leaves, they smell like shower curtain."

She took out what was in the clear pouch and unfolded it.

"It be a poncho!" she exclaimed. "A poncho with leaves all over it."

"Put it on," I said, "let me see how you look in it."

The hood of the poncho covered her hair with leaves, but showed her face. I noticed that when she kept her hands and arms under the poncho, the poncho turned everything between her shoulders and her knees into a leafy lump.

Flew looked like a bush with a human face; she did not look at all like a child wearing raingear.

She asked me, "Why you grinning so big?"

I replied, "Because that poncho is giving me half an idea. I can sneak up to the Corny Dog after I put the poncho on, and somehow get rid of all the Gluttons' pies. Well, I can sneak up as soon as I find out where the Gluttons and Poofa all are at."

Flew said, "The Gluttons, they back at the Corny Dog, so you be careful. But Poofa, I don't know where he at. I ain't seed him since him and Cakedough, they get into a fight."

Chapter 14
Skunk-Works

Right after I learned about Cakedough and Poofa getting into a fight, Flew and I were interrupted by "Pachelbel's Canon," then by Barnacle Brained's voice—

"Attention, contestants. Jose Marinas of School Zone Ten has been eliminated. Nine contestants remain."

"Who be left?" Flew asked, as she was taking off the leafy poncho. "Me, Thrash, you, Poofa, the three Gluttons . . ."

I said, "A boy from Three is working with the Gluttons. That makes eight."

"So who the ninth? I can't think of nobody else."

Neither could I. I shrugged, and decided that the ninth contestant probably did not matter.

Flew said to me, "Anyway, you want to get rid of all them Gluttons' pies at the Corny Dog? I like that! But how you gonna do it?"

I shrugged. "I'll figure it out when I get there. All I know now is, I'll be wearing this poncho."

"Whatever you do, the Gluttons gonna pie you right after. Before you take two steps."

I smiled evilly. "Then we have to make sure the Gluttons are somewhere else when I'm at the Corny Dog, right?"

Flew got quiet and thoughtful for a short time. Then she said, "What about I stand far away from the Corny Dog and scream my head off? When the Gluttons show up, then I climb a tree."

"*Or*," I said, "we try *this*."

I picked up Flew's police whistle. "You blow this, you give it everything you got. More people would hear it than would hear you scream."

"*And* my throat ain't gonna hurt none. I like that."

"Now we have a plan. We only have to figure out how I'll know the Gluttons haven't pieed *you*. I can't very well go around yelling and have you yell back."

Flew said, "I got an idea. My grandmother, she likes birds, so last year when I have to enter a project for Science Fair, I do my project on birdcalls."

"Is she the grandmother with the plum tree?"

"Yeah, she real sweet. Anyway, here my idea: You do a mockingbird call when you want to ask me, 'You okay?' and I answer back with my own mockingbird call."

Flew whistled a birdcall, then added, "The Gluttons hear it, they think it two mockingbirds talking."

I whistled the mockingbird call twice, till I got it right. But then I had a thought—

"What if a *real* mockingbird whistles instead of you? How will I know?"

"We add a blue jay." Flew repeated the mockingbird call, then whistled a different birdcall. "You whistle the mockingbird, then the blue jay; I answer back with the same. A bird, he gonna sing one birdcall or the other, not both."

I practiced whistling the mockingbird/blue-jay birdcalls till I had learned them.

"I *like* your idea, Flew," I said. "You're clever."

Flew grinned.

✳✳✳✳

One minute later, Flew was looking at me and giggling. Truth be told, she seemed unable to *stop* giggling.

Part of my plan, to destroy all the Gluttons' goodies, was to wear my pie-carry bag under my leafy poncho. I wasn't sure whether that was a smart idea or a stupid idea, but leaving the pie-carry bag behind was not an option. Nor was it an option to set the bag next to me on the ground while I spied on the Gluttons, because the Gluttons would spot the bag's red color.

So there I was, dressing for my dangerous mission while Flew watched. I put the pie-carry bag on over my apron, which meant messing with straps and buckles. Then I pulled the cowl of the leafy poncho over my head, and draped the rest of the leafy poncho over the rest of my shape—including the shape that the pie-carry bag made.

As soon as I did all this, Flew started giggling. Nonstop.

Between giggles, Flew managed to say, "Karen, you look so silly!"

I lifted my chin and kept my dignity. I reminded myself that I was a mature woman of sixteen.

****

When I was suited up, I said to Flew, "I'll meet you back here, inside that maintenance shed." I pointed to the Panem ISD red shed that was only a few yards away. "You'll get back here before I do, so please be patient."

Flew grinned. " 'Be patient'? Ain't happening, girlfriend! Soon as you walk through that door, I gonna be saying, 'Tell me what happen! Tell me what happen!' "

"That's fine," I said, "just don't wander around looking for me. You don't want to run into the Gluttons, especially if I've done something *unfriendly* to their hoard."

****

The Corny Dog's "meadow" was artificial. For one thing, the meadow was rectangular. For another thing, inside the rectangle, no plants grew except grass.

Weeds, wildflowers, bushes, shrubs, trees—all those other plants grew *outside* the meadow, though some came close to the boundary line.

Neither the Gluttons nor Three Boy reacted when the wild land near the meadow gained one more leafy thing.

By now, hours had passed since the gong. Empty backpacks were piled up at one spot on the meadow, while the Gluttons had gathered all their goodies at another spot.

Two yards or so from the Corny Dog, a checkered plastic tablecloth was spread on the ground. On that tablecloth, I saw the Pie Palanquin, bags of potato chips, canned foods, water bottles, and various odds and ends.

One of the oddball items was a spool of some kind of thin line—fishing line? Dental floss? Sewing thread? Laying on the tablecloth near the spool was a pair of scissors.

The plastic tablecloth was kept from blowing away by tent pegs. But for four corners, I saw *five* tent pegs; one corner had two pegs. This was puzzling.

The Gluttons were standing around at the stick-end of the Corny Dog—meaning, they were far away from their treasure hoard. To me, it seemed nobody was paying any attention to that part of the meadow, or to the land beyond the meadow.

What's stopping me from walking over and robbing them blind? This is way too easy.

I'm missing something.

Why did the Gluttons make that scrawny School Zone Three boy part of their group?

Three Boy was holding a pie casually in each hand, and his posture was relaxed. Meaning, he was not confronting the Gluttons. The Gluttons were relaxed too; they were not worried about Three Boy pieing them.

Maybe the deal he offered them was, "If I guard your stuff till the end, you don't pie me till the end."

But that isn't much of an offer. The Gluttons would've turned him down and pieed him on the spot. If he talked his way into the Pack, he had to have made a much better offer.

But what this better offer might be, I could not guess. Why the Gluttons were letting their goodies lay out in the open, I could not guess.

****

Five minutes later, I had been kneeling in that same spot, stumped by the mystery that I had not been able to solve.

Why are they leaving this stuff out in the open, where it's so easy to steal?

Behind me and to my right, I heard a police whistle: five long, loud blasts.

Garlic sing-songed, "Somebody's in trouble!"

Cakedough said, "Let's serve him pie."

Marblecake asked, "Could that be Poofa?"

Cakedough snorted. "Loverboy? C'mon. After what we *did* to him? If that turkey had a whistle, he would've been blowing it *long* ago."

Garlic said, "Why are we still gabbing?" She ran to the Corny Dog, grabbed two of the few pies that were still on top, ran back to the group, and handed a pie to Cakedough.

Marblecake, meanwhile, had grabbed a pie away from Three Boy.

Then Cakedough whirled around and pointed at Three Boy. "*You*—stay here."

With that, the three Gluttons ran toward the whistle-sound. Screaming as they ran, they were as loud as the police whistle they were running toward.

Once the Gluttons were gone, Three Boy walked over to the south end of the Corny Dog, straddled the "stick," and leaned back against the "dog."

Where Three Boy was sitting, he could not see the treasure trove at all.

He was either stupid, lazy, or confident.

I could not guess which.

****

Not ten seconds after Three Boy sat down, red-haired Firefox burst out of the trees to the left of me, by the fake lake. She sprinted across the meadow, then she slowed down to a walk, then—

Near the tablecloth, Firefox stopped.

While looking down, she lifted her left foot up several inches high, then set it down forward onto the tablecloth; then she brought her right foot up several inches high, then brought that foot forward and down next to her left foot.

Firefox was stepping over something.

Firefox pulled a plastic grocery bag out of a pocket of her apron. From the Gluttons' hoard, Firefox took a water bottle and two cans of food, quietly put them in her plastic bag, quietly tied the ends of the plastic bag together, and stuck the bag in her apron.

Firefox picked up a pie from the Pie Palanquin. Then she turned around, and again stepped over the whatever-it-was. Firefox jogged across the meadow and back to the trees.

I whispered, "It's booby-trapped."

****

Among the bounty on the checkered tablecloth was a handled cake-carrier. Or rather, the top of the cake-carrier. I hadn't bothered to look, presuming that the disk-shaped bottom to the cake-carrier was underneath the top.

Wrong. It turned out that the flat, round, white bottom of the cake-carrier was on the grass nearby. Actually, the cake-carrier bottom was tucked against the bottom side of the Corny Dog, where it was unlikely to be stepped-on or kicked.

Set on the cake-carrier bottom was an air horn, like at sporting events, with a pushbutton at the top.

Also set on the cake-carrier bottom, next to the air horn, was a big, flat rock. One end of the rock was propped up by a stick, so that this end of the rock was an inch above the air horn's pushbutton.

The stick that was holding one end of the rock up, seemed like it would fall over if you looked at it cross-eyed.

I was looking at a modified deadfall trap. Which made me wonder, *What will make that stick stop holding the rock up?*

The answer: fishing line. Once I knew what I had to look for, I saw it.

The tent pegs not only were holding the tablecloth down, they were stretching taut a loop of fishing line.

Walk onto that tablecloth without lifting your feet, and the fishing line gets jostled. Then the rock falls. Then the air horn blasts your eardrums. And before you can grab much of anything, the Gluttons (or their minion) are throwing pies at you.

****

The simple thing to do, since Three Boy was slacking off so hard, would be to run to the flat rock, lay the rock aside to disarm the alarm, then steal bunches of the Gluttons' stuff.

This assumed I had time to spare. But for all I knew, I was only seconds away from Three Boy spotting me.

I was trying to cook up a Plan B when I spotted the skunk. A cute beast, the skunk was black with twin white stripes and a fluffy tail, and the skunk's face was adorable.

Normally skunks only came out at night, but I guessed that the loud noises, nearby and recently, had awakened this skunk. Sleepiness was perhaps why the skunk was moving slowly across the ground.

I slowly walked up to the skunk. Since I could not read a skunk's expressions, I did not know if the skunk was alarmed or not.

I slowly squatted down. I still had no clue what the skunk was thinking.

Is the shower-curtain smell and my leafy covering confusing the skunk? I'm about to find out.

My hand came out from under the poncho, I reached under the skunk's body, and I stood up.

Please don't bite me or spray me, skunk!

Then I, with skunk in hand, ran for the pegged-down tablecloth as fast as I could go.

Alas, between the pie-carry bag, the poncho, and carrying a skunk in my right hand, my "fast" was poky.

While I'm strolling across the grass, will Three Boy see me and pie me?

Will I get skunk-bit? Or worse, skunk-nuked?

Or will I actually pull this off?

When I got close enough to the tablecloth, I gave the skunk an underhand toss.

Even while the skunk was still flying through the air, I hurried to back away out of range.

****

Everything worked even better than I had hoped—

The skunk landed on the edge of the top shelf of the Pie Palanquin, and the skunk's sideways momentum tipped over the Pie Palanquin. For the second time, I had managed to get the Pie Palanquin to dump all its pies.

Meanwhile, that skunk had been dumped on the ground, and the skunk was annoyed.

The skunk lifted its bushy tail and turned its body a full circle as it sprayed. The Pie Palanquin, the pies themselves, the potato chips, the cans of food, the water bottles, the fishing line, the scissors—all got skunk-nuked.

I was lucky—the skunk didn't stink me up at all.

By then, I was running toward the trees and wildflowers, my back to the skunk. For two seconds, I wondered if the skunk was only *pretending* to be angry; everything smelled normal. Then instantly, the meadow stank.

I was not ready for the *power* of that stink. It was the smell-same as someone revving a motorcycle only inches from my ear.

After the skunk showed the world that it did not like rude treatment, the animal tried to walk back to the forest.

The skunk bumped up against the fishing-line tripwire.

H-O-O-O-O-NK!

****

I thought, *I didn't get skunk-sprayed! I didn't get bit! The odds are in my favor.*

Not to mention—my trick worked!

Once again I wanted to high-five myself, because once again I had been a punishment for Gluttons.

Before I rejoined Flew, I *really* wanted to see the Gluttons react to my prank.

Chapter 15
Where Was Flew?

As soon as the air horn began to sound, Three Boy jumped up and ran a short ways with one pie in hand. He saw leafy-me running into the trees, but he did not chase me.

Seconds later, I ran back to where I was among the trees and wildflowers. There I turned to watch the meadow.

I saw two referees dash to the far end of the meadow, putting themselves as far away as they could get from the skunked hoard. Those referees were holding their noses as they talked on their radios.

The air horn *HONK*ed till it ran out of air, but Three Boy made no effort to stop the noise. He just stood there, close to both his deadfall trap and the skunk-smelling hoard; he looked worried.

A minute later, Marblecake, Cakedough, and Garlic ran panting into the meadow, each with a pie in hand. Then they changed direction and ran panting to stand by Three Boy.

When Garlic realized that the entire hoard had been skunk-sprayed, she cussed a blue streak.

"Damn," said Marblecake, "now I'll have to work harder to win."

Cakedough did not say a word. Instead, he slipped his own hand under Three Boy's pie-holding hand, then brought his hand up and back. *Splat.*

Three Boy fell to the ground.

Now only eight contestants were left.

****

Less than a minute later, the golf-cart driver had loaded unconscious Three Boy into his golf cart (with help from

Marblecake). As soon as the golf cart drove off, Marblecake slapped Cakedough on the back of his head. *Hard.*

"You dummy. You never gave him a chance to tell us about the skunker. You had to hurry and pie him, didn't you?"

"*That's* easily fixed," Cakedough said. He waddled off to where two referees were watching.

I could not hear what Cakedough and the referees were saying, but I could see that Cakedough was getting angrier each second. After a minute, Cakedough stomped back to where Marblecake and Garlic waited.

Cakedough said, "Stupid referees wouldn't tell us who the skunker is. They *did* tell us eight of us are left—how generous. When I asked where the eight of us were at, those assholes laughed in our face."

Marblecake said, "Eight left, not seven, means Three Boy didn't pie the skunker."

Garlic said, "You know what? I am royally miffed. Five kids are left who aren't us, and one of them is the skunker. We've still got pies atop the Corny Dog, and we've got three pies in our hands. I say, No more playing nice! *Right now*, let's hunt those kids down like the dogs they are. But don't you pie Fire Bitch, she's *mine.*"

Marblecake nodded. "We hunt. Let's go."

The Gluttons took off for the trees as a fast waddle.

I stopped eavesdropping then, to go meet up with Flew. I was suddenly in a hurry.

****

I had not moved far from the meadow when I heard laughter *in* the meadow.

"*Myuhahaha!*"

This puzzled me, because none of the Gluttons seemed like a person to laugh easily. Maybe a referee was laughing?

Slowly, cautiously, I moved back to where I could see the meadow.

"*Myuhahahahaa!*"

Firefox, smiling and laughing, stood by the skunk-sprayed plastic tablecloth. Her left hand was holding a pie, while her right hand was making a fist-pump.

"I can win, I can win!" Firefox said. Then she did a little dance. "Maybe this fall I'll be gobbling down strawberry shortcake in the school cafeteria, while I write my Great Novel on my laptop. Oh, I hope I'll have adventures to share at the Mensa party tonight!"

I toyed with the idea of walking out into the meadow and inviting Firefox to join our alliance.

But I quickly decided against it—something sounded *not quite right* about how she laughed.

Besides—

Firefox, I could tell, was left-handed. *And* she was a redhead. I had friends who were left-handed, and I had friends who were redheaded, but I had *no* friends who were both. (I was choosy about my friends.)

But the absolute deal-killer was learning that Firefox was redheaded *and* she was a fiction author. I firmly believe that red-haired authoresses are not to be trusted.

****

I successfully avoided the Gluttons as I rushed to the maintenance shed where I was to meet up with Flew.

I opened the maintenance-shed door, and walked in with a smile on my face. "Hey, Flew, here I—"

Flew wasn't here.

Maybe she slipped out to find a portable toilet. Good luck with that.

I sat down on a metal stool while I waited for her.

****

Half an hour later, I was racking my brain to come up with a Plan B; something was *very* wrong.

I pulled off my leafy poncho, jammed it into its clear plastic pouch, put the plastic pouch in my backpack (which still lay on a worktable), and walked with determination out of the maintenance shed. I still was wearing the pie-carry bag.

****

I was not a hunter. If I were, I could read the flattened grass and the broken twigs, and then I would know which way Flew had gone.

But since I was a city girl, I had to resort to walking a spiral search.

While praying that the Gluttons did not find me before I found Flew.

****

I made the mockingbird birdcall. I made the blue-jay birdcall. Then I listened.

Silence.

I spoke quietly: "Flew, if you can hear me, please answer me."

More silence, then I walked away.

****

Again I whistled the mockingbird birdcall; again I made the blue-jay birdcall.

Again the result was silence.

I was past *worried* now; I was *scared*. I wondered, *What has happened to Flew?*

I resumed walking.

****

The referee was standing under a pine tree. I hurried up to him and said, "Please tell me where Flew is at. The girl from School Zone Eleven."

The referee replied, "Sorry, I can't help you. Even if we knew where she was, I wouldn't tell you."

"What do you mean, 'Even if we knew'?"

"Forget I said that."

"She's wearing an ankle-tracker, *hello?* You know *exactly* where she is!"

The referee frowned. "In theory, yes. The fact is, we've lost her."

"You have to find her! I think she's in trouble."

He said, "Do you have any idea how many referees have been dispatched to this part of the woods? Just to spot one little girl?"

I sighed. "Then how about Poofa Meadowlark, the male from School Zone Twelve? Where is he now?"

The referee didn't bother to answer. He crossed his arms and looked at me with a raised eyebrow.

****

Ten minutes later, I made the mockingbird call; I made the blue-jay call.

Less than a second later, I heard matching sounds. They were coming from somewhere nearby but high above me.

Flew is okay!

****

Flew made mockingbird/blue-jay birdcalls, and I answered, as I moved closer to where Flew was.

I made mockingbird/blue-jay birdcalls, and Flew answered, as I moved closer to where Flew was.

I was now very close to Flew's hiding place when I heard a young girl's startled cry, then running feet, then a second pair of running feet.

A male voice yelled, "I have you now, little girl! Are you the skunker?"

Right at that moment, I saw something white and shiny under a tree. *Flew might have dropped this.*

As fast as the pie-carry bag would let me, I ran toward the shiny object.

It was a police whistle.

"KAREN! HELP!" Flew yelled.

I opened the flap of the pie-carry bag, grabbed a pie, and hurried toward Flew's voice.

As did two referees.

Chapter 16
I Sang To Flew

Marblecake was holding Flew's right wrist with his left hand, so that she could not run away. Marblecake was holding only one pie, but one was enough.

Splat.

From hairline to chin, from ear to ear, Marblecake's pie covered Flew's face with pie-goop.

Marblecake's back was to me. As I ran up close to him, I made my voice sound (almost) like Garlic's. "Wow, Marblecake, good frigging job."

He turned around, grinning.

Splat. I was standing so close, my hand still was pushing the pie when it hit his face.

From hairline to chin, from ear to ear, Marblecake's face also was covered with pie-goop.

Marblecake mumbled, "This can't be. I'm supposed to win." Then he dropped to the ground.

Flew still was standing up—but barely. She was swaying back and forth.

Now I noticed that a red ESPN camera and two referees were watching us. The referees walked up, then each briefly looked at the face of a pied contestant.

The older referee announced, "The School Zone One male and the School Zone Eleven female are eliminated." The younger referee started to talk on his radio.

I hugged wobbly Flew to me and said to the referees, "You can't eliminate her! She's still on her feet."

The younger referee put his radio back on his belt. "It's the pieing that eliminates her, not the fainting. She's out."

Sure enough, "Pachelbel's Canon" played; Barnacle Brained announced the two eliminations and announced that the contestants were down to six.

Both referees walked away then, but the red, roving TV camera still was aimed at Flew and me.

"Karen?" Flew said. "I feel real sleepy."

****

Flew frowned. "I hide in that tree because I hear people walking around. I think they Gluttons—but no, they all referees. And when at last I come down from that tree, I do it when that Glutton, he see me. I a fool."

"Shh. You're not a fool."

"You destroyed their stuff?"

"Smell that skunk-stink? The Gluttons' stuff, I got it skunk-sprayed. Every last bit."

Flew's eyes were still open, and she still was talking, but now she was limp in my arms. I pulled off her backpack, laid her on the ground, then I sat down beside her.

As I was using my hands to wipe pie-goop off of Flew's face, she said, "You have to win."

"I'm going to. Going to win for both of us now."

"We don't got much time left. You a good girlfriend."

For some reason, this made me cry.

Flew said, "Please sing for me. You sing so pretty."

"No problem, Flew," I said, choking back a sob.

A golf cart had driven up. Now the driver got out, walked up to me, and tapped me on the shoulder. "Can you hurry up whatever you're doing?" he demanded in a deep voice. "I got places to be!"

"Be patient!" I snapped. "Flew asked me to sing to her."

****

Thick, siz-zle-ling steak,
Cut with steak knife agleam,
With it, big taters,
Filled with tart sour cream,
Where you are going, the food tastes so good.

Think of fried chicken,
Crispy, it is so hot,
With big buttered rolls
(Or) cornbread—hot, quite a lot,
Where you are going, the food tastes so good.

Then the golf-cart driver surprised me: He started to sing *Bim-bam, oomie-chukka, oomie-chukka, oomie-chukka,* in bass harmony to my melody!

Add in fresh pizza,
Grab a wide, steaming slice,
Taste meats, cheeses, and
Veggies, peppery spice.
Where you are going, the food tastes so good.

By now the branches around us were heavy with birds of every color and size. (I thought I saw blue jays.) The birds added three-part soprano/alto harmonizing with me—

Salty brown pretzels,
Chips with ranch-flavor dip,
Buttered hot popcorn—
Snacks to taste-please the lip,
Where you are going, the food tastes so good.

Then a skunk wandered up. The skunk gave me a drop-dead look, but then added a tenor line to the last verse—

Finish with sweet stuff,
Taste that rich choc'late cake,

Kin back together,
Dead dogs play by the lake,
Where you are going, each moment is good.

By now, Flew was unconscious, and tears ran down my face.

By now, the golf-cart driver, all the singing birds, the skunk, and even some fluffy bunnies—they all were dancing around Flew and me. But when my singing ended, the dancers all suddenly stopped.

****

The verse ended; "Food In Heaven" ended; three seconds of silence passed.

Then the golf-cart driver said, "*Now* can I take her?"

I bent down, kissed Flew's forehead, then whispered, "Not yet."

"*WHAT?*"

Wildflowers were growing only a few feet away. I picked a handful, while the golf-cart driver looked at me in confusion.

Then I laid them on the ground around Flew's head, to give her a halo of flowers—

"You're *nuts*, girl!"

—or at least, such was my plan. Alas, I had laid down only five wildflowers when the golf-cart driver glared at me, scooped up limp Flew, and carried her to the golf cart.

I stood up then, faced the ESPN camera and, while holding each hand aloft—

I gave back the one-fingered special gesture that the kids of School Zone Twelve had given me this morning. I hoped that School Zone One saw it clearly.

Meanwhile, the golf-cart driver was struggling to bring unconscious Marblecake to the golf cart—

I thought, *Good luck with that.* Marblecake, I was sure, weighed at least three times what Flew weighed.

I yelled to the golf-cart driver, "Your job would be easier if you took off his backpack and gave it to me."

The golf-cart driver stopped everything he was doing, in order to glare at me.

"What's your problem?" I said. "It's not like Big Boy here is going to *need* that backpack, is he?"

When at last I left the spot where Flew had been pieed, I had Marblecake's backpack hanging off my shoulders, and had Flew's light backpack laying atop my pie-carry bag.

****

I walked back to the tree where I had seen Flew's police whistle laying on the ground. I picked up the whistle and put it in a pocket of my apron.

****

Right after that, I heard a *THUP-THUP-THUP-THUP* sound. It was coming from above.

A drone helicopter, painted silver, dropped through an opening in the trees and then flew toward me. A few feet from me, the silver helicopter hovered in place.

A synthetic voice said, "Open me."

On the side-body of the helicopter was a rectangular door, outlined in blue, that was marked *Cargo*. I opened the door and found two things inside.

When I brought them out into the light, I discovered that they were a vacuum-packed package of beef jerky, and half of the front page of the PMS 11-C school newspaper.

As soon as I had closed the Cargo door, the drone helicopter took off.

When I had left the place where Flew had been pieed, which was the same place I had sung to her, a red ESPN camera had followed me. It was following me now. I turned to face the camera, and I held up the beef jerky. "My thanks to the people of School Zone Eleven," I said.

Then I sat down on the grass, planning to open up the packaging and snack on the jerky. *How many hours has it been since I've eaten anything?*

There was a place on the right side of the beef-jerky packaging where the packaging swerved in, with a little red ribbon sticking out. I knew that I was supposed to grab that red ribbon, and lift up and to the left; the ribbon would tear a line in the top of the packaging.

The only problem was, that red ribbon was greasy. When I pulled hard on the red ribbon, my fingers just slid off of it.

I tried this three times, and got the same result each time. *Who says I'm smart?*

The fourth time, I held my thumb and index finger a little differently, so that the red ribbon was pinched between two fingernails. I pulled, and my fingers didn't slide off the ribbon. *Victory for Twelve Girl!*

Not so: The tension in the ribbon suddenly dropped to zilch, my hand zoomed right, and now I was holding five inches of unattached red ribbon in my hand.

Bleep!

I laid the no-longer-useful ribbon on the half-page of newsprint, and attacked that package of jerky the hard way.

Since the front and back plastic walls were pressed tight against the jerky, there was no slack or looseness anywhere. I discovered quickly that I couldn't grab the front plastic wall between thumb and index finger, and the back plastic wall between thumb and index finger, and pull the bag apart.

Next, I tried gripping part of the packaging with both hands, then one hand moved toward me, while the other hand moved away. That trick worked to tear several pages of paper in half, right? Alas, the plastic packaging, where it was melted together, was so thick that I could not tear it.

After that, I tried biting the packaging, with bites making a rip that I could tear further. This got me no success, *and* I was sure I looked ridiculous on camera.

I was stuck with needing a knife or scissors. I pawed through Marblecake's backpack, and then Flew's backpack. No knife to be found; no scissors.

Then I remembered that I had seen scissors recently! The scissors were—

—next to the Corny Dog. Where Cakedough and Garlic might return to, at any time.

Not to mention, *these* scissors were skunk-sprayed. Did I *really* want to handle them, *and* get them near food that I planned to eat?

I looked at the ESPN camera and said, "People of School Zone Eleven, *ahem*, I'm not really hungry now. I'll eat your beef jerky later."

****

In School Zone Twelve, I was not considered to be a friendly person; and Primmy and Soozin were the only people who had ever seen me smile since my father had died. But I had never been considered to be an *angry* person.

But now I was angry—no, furious—no, *enraged*—at Cakedough and Garlic.

As I was walking back to the maintenance shed where I had left my leafy poncho and my own backpack, I craved to make those two be miserable.

If Cakedough or Garlic had appeared nearby, I would have charged the Glutton at a full run, and thrown pies till I had no more pies left, or either the Glutton was on the ground or I was.

If I stumbled on *both* Gluttons together, two against one, I would attack them in just as much of a berserker rage as I would attack only one—and if I got pieed, "Such is life."

Thrash or Firefox, if I found one of them, would get slightly more polite treatment, but not much. Because my attitude right now was, *Is Karen Ebergrimm the only contestant willing to take on Garlic and Cakedough, the Prince and Princess of Whales?*

I realized that the only remaining contestant that I would not pie on sight was Poofa.

Where is Poofa, anyway?

****

When I returned to the red maintenance shed, I went through Marblecake's knapsack. I found—

Lots of snack bars, two bottles of water, and this was pretty much it. Except for some cheap plastic binoculars and a National Weather Service radio that told Colorado weather.

I could not decide whether I was disgusted or envious. *It must be nice: The Piemakers put out stuff for twenty-four contestants, but only six contestants get to enjoy it, and they don't need to haul their bounty with them.*

But then I smiled. *If Cakedough and Garlic packed as light as Marblecake did, they have problems now!*

****

I refilled my pie-carrier bag in the maintenance shed, then wandered far away from the maintenance shed so that the Gluttons would not find that shed and its pies.

While I was leaning against a shady tree, I pulled my backpack off my back, and took from it Marblecake's snack bars. I took Flew's police whistle out of my apron pocket.

Between bites of snack bar, I played "Jingle Bells" on the police whistle.

Here I am, Gluttons. Now home in on the police whistle, then let's all dance.

A police whistle, I found out, is not a flute. A police whistle is much louder than a flute; and a flute can play many different notes, while a police whistle has only one pitch.

In short, my performance of "Jingle Bells" on the police whistle would not have impressed even Primmy.

But amazingly, no Gluttons showed up to trash-talk my musical skills.

Are the Gluttons afraid of me now? Whoa! But wait— maybe they think it was Thrash who was the skunker. The Gluttons might not want to battle Thrash till they had to, even two against one.

In any case, I blew that whistle and blew that whistle, letting the other five contestants know that somebody was right here; but no other contestant showed his face.

Chickens, all of you! AWK-buk-buk-buk-AWK!

****

While I was waiting for any other contestant to show up for my police-whistle recital, I realized two things—

I realized that Marblecake had been the third person I had pieed, but he had been the first time I had looked in someone's eyes when I had pieed them. (Four Girl's face had been in profile when I had pieed that face, and Glandular's eyes had been shut.)

The *big* thing I realized: I could *win* the Dessert Games. I was no longer an unarmed contestant trying to dodge fat kids with pies—no, I had pies of my own, I knew where I could get more, plus I was a girl on a mission.

****

The speakers played the same trumpet fanfare that had announced the wall of firetrucks.

Barnacle Brained then announced: "We have changed the rules. If the last two contestants in the Elimination are from the same school zone, both contestants will be declared winners. Good luck to the contestants from Two and Twelve."

What did he say?

I did not give a thought that Cakedough and Garlic might be lurking nearby, plotting something nasty. I did not give a thought about sneaky Firefox or about dangerous Thrash.

Instead, I yelled as loud as I could, *"POOFA!"*

Chapter 17
Cursed With Cooties

I had to find Poofa. *Right now.*

All I knew about where Poofa might be, was where he had been when I had pieed Glandular and Four Girl; and after that, Cakedough had done something bad to Poofa.

What did I do first to find Poofa? I took a quick walk.

It was easy to find the spot where I had ambushed Glandular and Four Girl, because there was plenty of pie-goop and pie pans by one particular tree.

But once I was standing at that spot, I was out of ideas. I could not begin to guess where Poofa had gone from here.

What do I know about Poofa that is unique? Maybe I can find him by how he is unique. How is Poofa different from every other boy I know?

One, he knows more about makeup than I do.

Two, he smells like fresh-baked bread. That is, except when he cleans up Sumbitch's vomit.

****

Remembering that Poofa smelled like fresh bread was when I thought up an idea how I could find Poofa.

I remembered that the maintenance shed where I had been recently, had a soldering iron and solder. With a little inventiveness, I could convert Marblecake's weather radio into a bread-smell detector. Then I could walk straight to wherever Poofa was.

Wow, I am so smart sometimes!

You dummy, you are so stupid sometimes. Rewiring the electronics in that radio would not be a quick job. And what if

I goofed up? What if my modified gizmo smelled unwashed socks instead of fresh-baked bread? *How embarrassing.*

That's when I got *an even better* idea how to find Poofa.

I rushed back to the maintenance shed only long enough to hang Flew's backpack from my left shoulder. Then I *rushed* away from the maintenance shed, in a new direction—

Rushed meaning here, *moved as fast as I could while wearing a full pie-carry bag, and wearing two backpacks that kept shifting around and smacking my elbows.* If anyone were watching me now, they probably were falling-down laughing.

****

The troll was at the same place—that is, under the same bridge—where I had left him.

But this time, I wasn't trying to act nasty to the troll. Instead, I was making him an offer—

One of my hands held out the zip-lock bag full of berries. The other hand was holding out the can of cocktail wieners. I said, "And all you have to do is help me find a boy who smells like bread."

"How old is this boy?" the troll asked.

"Sixteen, same age as me."

"Too old to eat, then."

"If I thought you were going to eat him, I wouldn't ask you to find him!"

The troll eyed the bag. "Are those berries poisonous?"

"C'mon, do I look like someone who carries poisonous berries around?"

"Why *me*, human girl? Why not ask another human?"

"The stories say that a troll can smell hiding children. I figure if you can smell children, you can smell bread."

"But I don't *like* bread! The only time I ever eat bread is when I make toddler sandwiches."

"But you know what fresh bread smells like. So you can find Poofa."

"Maybe I can, maybe I can't. A bag of berries and a little bit of meat isn't enough to make up for me maybe embarrassing myself. What else can you add?"

I sighed my best soap-opera sigh, as I dropped my offerings into Flew's backpack. "Thanks for your time. If you can't find him, I'll cook up some other plan."

I started to zip up Flew's backpack.

"*Wait!*" the troll said. "I maybe can find him; I'm just not *sure* I can find him. But still, I accept your offer."

"Great, let's go," I said.

****

In less than five minutes, the troll had led me to an outdoor, sunken hot tub that was surrounded by trees. A blond-haired teen boy sat on the rim of the hot tub, with his back to us. The blond boy was bent forward, so that his face was almost in the water.

I murmured to the troll, "I'm sure that's Poofa."

I then paid the troll the treats I had promised him.

As the troll was walking away, he said, "It's one thing to write that a fiction character is from Appalachia. But if you read her *aloud* as *talking* like people from Appalachia, then she sounds stupid."

Yep, I thought, *he's definitely a troll.*

****

"Poofa!" I said, behind him.

At the hot tub, Poofa did not turn around, speak, or gesture.

I hurried forward till I was standing by the other side of the hot tub, facing him. "I found you. I'm so glad."

He straightened up enough to look in my eyes. His face looked . . . *panicked?* "Don't come closer, Karen! *Stay away!*"

"You don't understand—they changed the rules. We can both win!"

"I HAVE COOTIES!"

"*What?* No, you don't. For one thing, I would have noticed your cooties on the bus."

"It's the truth. Remember right after you pieed Glandular and Marina? When I stopped pretending to be a Glutton and I told you I'd protect you from the Gluttons?"

"Of course I remember, but what does that have to do with cooties?"

"Cakedough got angry with me. He punched me in the nu—in a delicate place. That's when he also gave me *cooties!*"

Now I noticed that red-metallic insects were crawling over every part of Poofa's body that was out of the water.

I also noticed that Poofa's hair was a different color, no longer goldenrod exactly, and his hair had a little less luster. Also, Poofa's voice sounded slightly more nasal.

I must be imagining things.

I shook my head. "Poofa, these must be some other bug you've got. One, you don't get cooties after you hit puberty; and Two, a *boy* doesn't get cooties from another *boy.*"

"He does if the boy is unpopular enough! Does Cakedough strike you as a kid whom other kids in Two want to hang out with?"

"Well, if they *are* cooties, and you *did* catch them from Cakedough—"

I brought my right hand up, and pointed at it with my left index finger. "Circle, circle, dot, dot"—I used my left finger to draw those things on my right hand as I spoke—"now I have my cooties shot."

I walked around the hot tub toward Poofa, holding my hands out in front of me. As I got near Poofa, all the cooties hurriedly crawled to the far side of his body.

Which meant my body was now poison to cooties. Good, I had one less problem on this crazy afternoon.

I said, "Just you wait, Cakedough, till I tell the referees what you did to—"

"The Piemakers forgot to make a rule against hitting. This is legal."

"*Legal*, maybe, but it sure isn't *fair*."

Poofa looked at me with despair. "What am I supposed to do, Karen? I can't go back to PHS Twelve with cooties. I *sure* can't work in my dad's bakery with cooties!"

I said, "Let me think."

****

I walked halfway around the hot tub. I took off my pie-carry bag, my backpack, and Flew's backpack, and laid them on the hot-tub walkway. Now Poofa could reach them if the Gluttons or Thrash attacked us.

Then I again walked halfway around the hot tub, took off shoes and socks, and walked into the hot tub.

I can't believe I'm wading into a hot tub, fully dressed! Aloud, I said, "Poofa, I need for you to move here to where I'm standing. The middle of the hot tub."

Poofa seemed leery. "What do you plan to do?"

Even so, Poofa did trust me enough to slide all the way into the hot tub, and then he moved over to me.

I put my hand on his shoulders. "I'm going to dunk you under the water and drown the cooties. Take a deep breath and relax."

" 'Relax'? I still hurt where Cakedough punched m—*hey!*"

I held him under water for twenty seconds, then let him come back up. Metallic-red cooties floated to the water's surface, but none of them were swimming.

Poofa glared at me. "You made my makeup run."

"I'm trying to get you *clean*, Poofa! Even if it takes me hours."

A cootie crawled out of Poofa's apron, climbed up his neck, and ran into his hair.

Two seconds later, a second cootie crawled out of the collar of Poofa's t-shirt and soon was running over his face.

After I had seen my sixth cootie survive, I said, "Take another deep breath."

Gurgle. This time I held Poofa underwater for thirty seconds.

"Give me more of a warning next time!" he said, as soon as I let him come up. "I almost drowned!"

More dead cooties were floating on the surface of the water, so I hoped that this time, I had killed—

Two cooties crawled out of Poofa's t-shirt and onto his face at the same time.

****

I always won the hand-slap game with Primmy because I could move my hands fast. So I got the idea of snatching up cooties and crushing them between my fingernails.

My idea sort-of worked. But those rotten cooties kept ducking inside Poofa's t-shirt or apron, or in his hair.

I sighed. "Now we try Plan C."

****

Poofa looked at me warily. "What's Plan C?"

"Take off your apron, your t-shirt, and your shoes and socks."

"Say *what?*"

"Less clothing means fewer air pockets for the cooties."

Poofa threw his clothing toward me, where it all floated on the surface of the water. I drowned his clothing by pulling it underwater, and then by stepping on it for good measure.

I noticed that Poofa, when naked to the waist, had bulging shoulders and biceps; and his chest and stomach muscles weren't shabby either. I liked looking at half-undressed Poofa.

When Poofa was down to pants and underwear, he said, "The cooties still have two hiding places. I should take *everything* off."

"*No!*"

"Why not?" he asked, grinning.

"Because . . . because you'll get arrested! Indecency."

"No sweat if you testify at my trial," he replied cheerfully. He unsnapped his pants.

I quickly turned my back on him. I said, "If you insist on doing this, cover yourself with Flew's backpack."

"Gotcha. . . .Ow, ow, ow."

"What's wrong?" I called over my shoulder.

"One part of me hurts, and when I'm taking off pants and shorts, *that part* is right in the heat of the action."

"Poor you. Imagine getting punched in the jewels every thirty days—this is what menstrual cramps feel like."

Soon twin splashes at my elbows told me that Poofa was naked.

I dunked the pants with no problem, but when I got my hands on his briefs—

"You're kidding me. A sixteen-year-old boy wearing *Yellow-Caped Hero* underwear?"

"Hey, Yellow-Caped Hero stands for 'Honor, Right, Kindness, and Truth.' Those are good things to live by."

As I was drowning Poofa's underwear, I called over my shoulder, "You'll have to dunk yourself underwater by yourself. I won't do it for you."

Poofa's voice said cheerily, "I have to put Flew's backpack aside, then. Don't turn around or you'll see Poofa Junior."

I heard sloshing sounds. Then Poofa's voice called out— again with disgusting cheerfulness—"I'm still naked, and now I'm dipped. You know, you're kind of prudish for such an inventive person."

I dredged up Poofa's pants and shorts, then tossed them over my shoulder. "Cover yourself."

"Yes, *ma'am!*" Poofa's voice replied.

But a few seconds later, Poofa's voice was no longer cheery: "Aw, nuts."

"Are you in pain again?"

"Yeah, but that isn't the problem. I see cooties on the walkway around the hot tub, and now they're jumping back onto me. You got a Plan D?

"Let me thi—"

"*I* have a plan. But Karen, you won't like it."

****

I asked, "Why won't I like it?"

Poofa's voice replied, "Here's a hint: One of those red camera-cars just showed up. We're being watched."

"You haven't told me why I won't like it."

"I'm decent; you can turn around now." When I was again facing Poofa, he added, "We hug and kiss, and the cooties will be programmed to swarm you. But since you've had your cooties shot, as soon as they touch you—"

"—they'll die," I said.

I thought, *I never have kissed a boy before. I absolutely never have kissed a boy while ESPN was filming me.*

What would Soozin say if he saw this?

But Poofa needs for me to do this now.

Besides, Poofa has one muscular body above the belt.

Before I lost my nerve, I waded over to where Poofa was standing, I took his face in my hands, and I kissed him.

I kissed Poofa as hotly as I had seen that blond Louisville actress ever kiss anyone in a movie.

My hot kiss did the trick: Cooties crawled briefly onto me, fell off, and sizzled when they hit the water.

****

After I kissed Poofa, the cooties seemed completely gone.

What was even better: By the time Poofa had gotten dressed, a silver drone helicopter had delivered to us an easy-open can of chicken broth, plus two paper cups.

I smiled at Poofa. "*Ha*, proof that Sumbitch likes me. Am I good, or what?"

Poofa said, "Actually, it's clear that Sumbitch can't stand you. Maybe because of your charm and grace, or lack thereof?" Poofa was smiling as he said that.

I smiled back. "No charm or grace, huh? I'll show *you*."

With that, I kissed Poofa again. This kiss, however, was only PG-rated.

As Poofa looked dazed and happy, I said, "I know a place where we can eat this without the Gluttons bothering us."

Poofa said, "Someplace *private?* Oh, wow." Poofa looked at me with starry eyes, which I ignored.

I did not figure in my plans that with Poofa's groin pain, he could only limp slowly. Our walk from the hot tub to the maintenance shed was taking *way* too long; I worried that

Cakedough and Garlic would catch us out in the open and pie us. Still, we managed to avoid everyone else.

Correction: We avoided *almost* everyone else. An ESPN camera-car followed us, and a referee walked up to us.

****

The referee was walking from Someplace to Someplace Else, which put him walking close to us as we trudged toward the red maintenance shed.

"Good afternoon, contestants," the referee said politely. Then he did a double-take.

At first, I thought the referee had noticed our soaking-wet clothing. Nope.

The referee was eyeing Poofa's apron. "Contestant, is that a *cootie* I see?"

"*What?*" I said. "Where?"

I looked. Sure enough, a red-metallic cootie was lying on Poofa's apron. But it was not moving. I flicked it away.

I looked up to see that the referee was glaring at me.

"Don't blame me," I said.

"She's right," Poofa said. "Cakedough punched me in the nuts. He gave me cooties at the same time."

The referee made a face.

I said, "Still, I think we got them all."

I added, blushing, "Poofa figured out a trick that seems to kill them."

The referee grabbed his walkie-talkie and said, "I have to call this in."

"You do that," I replied. "And tell Barnacle Brained to make Cakedough's stunt illegal next year."

The referee hurried away then, talking quietly into his walkie-talkie. I could not hear what he was saying.

****

When we walked into the red maintenance shed, Poofa said, "It has pies!"

"*And* electricity, *and* lights, *and* a worktable, *and* a soldering iron and solder, *and* a little window, so we can check the weather outside."

Poofa pointed. "We don't need the window for that." The wall opposite the door had a knothole in it; I saw grass.

The chicken broth was not much to eat, and it sure was not fancy, but it *was* food, and we both were hungry. After each of us drank our half-can of broth, we both got sleepy.

We lay down on the floor of the maintenance shed and napped.

****

"Karen, wake up," Poofa murmured.

My first though when I woke up was, *Poofa sounds like he caught a cold.*

I asked, "What's wrong?"

He whispered, "Sunlight is still coming through the window. But that knothole, it's dark. We're being watched."

I raised my head and looked. Sure enough, beyond the knothole was darkness.

"Stay here," I said, "I'll be right back."

I walked out, and solved the mystery: A red ESPN camera was playing Peeping Tom through the knothole.

When I walked back in the maintenance shed, I gasped—

Poofa's face and arms were crawling with red-metallic cooties.

Chapter 18
A Purple Unicorn, Many Orange Daisies

"Why are you staring at me?" Poofa asked, as I shut the shed's door.

Poofa's voice definitely sounded nasal. His voice was higher pitched, too. He sounded like one of Soozin's role-playing-game friends, not like Poofa of this morning.

And there was something else—

I reached for the maintenance shed's light switch. When I could see Poofa better, I gasped again.

There were two zits on Poofa's face that I was *sure* had not been on his face at the hot tub.

"Karen, you're worrying me," Poofa said. "Why are you staring at me?"

His hair—it had no shininess at all now, and its yellow color had faded to dinginess.

I answered his question with horror in my voice: "Your voice is different now. Your hair is different now. You have zits. And your cooties are back!"

"Oh, is that all? Snort-snort"—*bleep*, even Poofa's laugh sounded nerdy now—"and here I thought it was something serious. Like my leg being sliced open to the bone and blood poisoning setting in."

"Stop joking!" I said. "We have to fix this!"

Quickly, I dropped to my knees. I slipped a hand under Poofa's head, I yanked him up to a sitting position, and I kissed him.

Or rather, I tried to.

It was *not* a hot kiss. It was if I had to kiss one of Soozin's nerdy friends. A big part of the problem was, Poofa did not smell like baked bread anymore, he smelled like vinegar.

When I broke the lukewarm kiss, only three dead cooties lay on the floor.

I gasped yet again, when I realized: "The cooties are changing you! Making you so they can't be killed."

"Changing me how?"

"They're making you *unpopular*, so no girl will give you hot kisses that will kill cooties."

He shrugged. "You're the only girl I've ever loved. I don't care what other girls think of me."

"*You* might not care whether you have cooties, but *I* do! I will *not* let these bugs turn you into another Cakedough!"

Then I got a horrible thought. I said, "Stand up, stand up!" as I myself stood.

Poofa no longer was taller than me; now he was three inches shorter than me. Also, his shoulders looked wrong.

I put my hands on Poofa's shoulders. As I had feared, his shoulders were not as wide as when he had been half-naked at the hot tub. His arms weren't as muscular, and his stomach no longer was flat.

I growled, then I declared, "I refuse to accept this!"

****

Poofa replied, "So I have a real problem now. Nuts, I can't think about this. Please, let's talk about anything else."

"Like what?"

"Like . . . like, what is your favorite color? Mine is sunset orange."

I answered, "My favorite color is green. The color of dandelion leaves."

"Why dandelion leaves? Why *that* green?"

"Dandelion-leaf green reminds me of the first time Primmy patted her full stomach, after I got money for something I'd invented."

"Huh." Poofa paused a few seconds. "Tell me about the happiest day you can remember."

"That's easy. That would be the day I bought Lady, Primmy's pygmy mulberry-colored unicorn."

"Huh. Why a pygmy unicorn, instead of one full-sized?"

"A pygmy unicorn is small enough that a little girl can ride it, and a back yard has enough grass to feed the pygmy unicorn. But do you know what is *special* about a mulberry-colored unicorn?"

"Nope, I can't begin to guess."

"A regular unicorn will gore you with its horn if you try to touch it, it you aren't—"

"I, *ahem*, don't have to worry about that. I qualify, you get me? Go on with your story."

I said, "Um, I qualify too. But for a mulberry unicorn to let you touch it, you also have to be *nice*. Primmy is nice; I'm *not* nice. So the only way—"

"What do you mean, you're not nice? If you weren't nice, I wouldn't love you."

"I tried to drown Primmy's cat when he was a kitten, okay? I'm not a nice person. So the only way I could get that pygmy mulberry-colored unicorn home was by pulling on a ten-foot-long rope that the unicorn-wrangler gave me."

"So how did you get the money?" Poofa asked. "I'm sure that a pygmy mulberry-colored unicorn wasn't cheap."

****

A trumpet fanfare sounded, then Barnacle Brained interrupted to announce—

"Attention, contestants. In an hour, there will be a Feast at the Corny Dog. We will offer tasty food there, enough for all six of you."

I shook my head. I had no interest in potato chips and pizza, not when Poofa still had his cooties-problem. Not to mention, now was *not* the time to risk getting eliminated by Cakedough or Garlic—not when Poofa needed me.

I forgot that ESPN was filming Poofa and me through the knothole. The entire USA maybe saw me shake my head.

Barnacle Brained certainly did—

"Now hold on, if you're planning on skipping the Feast. We also will be offering special medicine that Cakedough, Garlic, and Poofa all need desperately. Also, we will give out fifty-dollar Wal-Mart gift certificates to Firefox and Thrash."

I thought, *Garlic has cooties too? Serves her right.*

Then I realized: *If the Piemakers are offering cooties-medicine for Poofa, I have to be at that Feast.*

Unfortunately, Poofa did the math and came up with the same number: "Forget it, Karen. Shove the idea of going to the Feast right out of your head."

"What baloney. I was planning no such thing."

"Your pants are on fire, Karen."

"*Fine*, I'm *going*, and you can't stop me!"

"If you go, then I'll follow after you, shouting your name so everyone knows you're coming."

I replied with a death-glare.

We went around and around like this for the next half-hour. Poofa insisted that I stay at the maintenance shed; I insisted that he needed for me to go to the Feast.

Our argument was interrupted then by the sound of a drone helicopter. I went outside to claim the bounty.

What Sumbitch had sent me was a small, "travel-sized" bottle of Acme Chloroform.

I was trying to figure out how to use Sumbitch's gift when I noticed, *really* noticed, my surroundings.

Fifteen yards from the maintenance shed was a tiny garden, not quite 20 square feet, that was walled off by railroad ties. In that garden grew daisies, but *these* daisies had bright-orange petals and brown centers.

I ran over to the garden. I picked flowers. Then I opened up the bottle of chloroform and dumped the strange-smelling liquid all over the orange daisies in my hand.

Seconds later, I walked inside, grinning. "Poofa, look! Sumbitch sent you a bouquet of daisies, and they're your favorite color. You *gotta* smell them, they smell so good!"

"Really? Let me see! Let me smell!"

I handed Poofa the orange daisies. Poofa sniffed the flowers—and almost instantly, he was unconscious.

Still, there was enough time after Poofa sniffed the doctored flowers for him to realize what the truth was. Just before Poofa's eyes shut, they were glaring daggers at me.

Chapter 19
Feasting And Pieing

I left a water bottle and a lemon-meringue pie on the floor of the maintenance shed, where Poofa could reach them if he needed them.

While I was kneeling next to Poofa, I bent down and gave him a long, lingering kiss. My motivation? Most of it was for us to look good for the camera. But not all of it.

Then I stood up, walked to the worktable, made sure my pie-carry bag was full of pies, pulled the pie-carry bag on me, and cinched the straps down tight. I walked out the door.

I wished I could disguise the maintenance shed. If something bad happened to me so that I did not return here, nothing stopped another contestant from walking in and pieing unconscious Poofa. *Bleep*, there were even available pies on the worktable for the contestant to throw!

Alas, my invisibility machine still did not work right—and in any case, I had not thought of bringing the prototype with me to this morning's Selection. So making the maintenance shed invisible was not an option.

The only other idea I could think of, was to drape the doorway of the maintenance shed with fake Halloween cobwebs. This way, another contestant would think that there was nothing inside, but Poofa could still walk out the door. Unfortunately, Halloween cobwebs could be bought only at Halloween, and Halloween was now months away.

So with a sigh, I walked away from the undisguised red maintenance shed, as I hoped for Poofa's safety. Next stop: the Corny Dog.

****

As I walked amid trees, bushes, and wildflowers, I had time to think.

And what I thought was, *Is Soozin watching all this on cable? What does he think of all the times I've kissed Poofa?*

I wondered if Soozin and I were finished as a couple. Then I wondered if he and I had ever been a couple. Then I wondered whether I wanted for Soozin and I to start being a couple when I returned. Certainly Soozin was nice to look at.

Then I wondered what kind of girl I was. When I had kissed Poofa, I had enjoyed it; but five minutes later, I was wondering what kissing Soozin would be like. *I'm a tramp.*

****

Minutes later, I was at the edge of the tree line, looking out at the rectangular meadow and the Corny Dog.

The first thing I noticed was Firefox, lying on her stomach on the ground near the Corny Dog. What I could see of the side of her face had pie-goop on it, and a splattered pie lay on the grass nearby. Firefox's breathing was slow and calm.

It's funny how I didn't hear either the classical-music song or the announcement that Firefox had been eliminated.

I shrugged. *I have been distracted this past hour.*

The second thing I noticed was that everything that had been skunk-sprayed was gone. I sniffed, and realized that the skunk-smell was now barely noticeable.

A worker in white coveralls was laying out replacement pies atop the Corny Dog. The Corny Dog was now as "armed" as when the gong had sounded.

On the lake (left) side of the meadow, I saw three referees and a golf cart waiting. On the opposite side of the meadow from me, I saw three more referees, and one more golf cart. On the right side of the meadow, I saw yet another three referees and one more golf cart. I presumed that my side of the meadow continued this three-and-one trend, but I was not willing to stick my head out past the tree line and check.

Something bothered me about seeing all those referees and golf carts standing idle. Something did not add up.

Not counting Firefox and me (and Poofa), three other contestants were either already here or were coming soon. But I saw none of them.

On my side of the Corny Dog was a big blue tent. Golf carts that carried food were parked in front of this tent, and Panem ISD workers were carrying food and other things inside the tent. A wide tent flap was hanging down, so that I could not see what was inside the tent.

I still could not shake the feeling that I was overlooking something, that somehow I was being tricked.

Suddenly the Panem ISD workers were done. All but two of the workers left, and all but one of the food-hauler golf carts left. Those two workers took up stations on each side of the tent flap.

Now the referees moved in. Three referees moved to stand in front of the tent flap. The two school-district workers rolled the tent flap up, tied the tent flap so it would not come down, then they drove off in their golf cart.

A referee spoke into a walkie-talkie.

I realized what was bothering me: *If so many referees and golf carts are here standing around, why hasn't Firefox already been—*

A fanfare sounded; Barnacle Brained's voice announced, "Attention, contestants. Let the Feast begin!"

****

One second later, "pieed" Firefox was on her feet and running toward the blue tent, as the referees were moving aside. Seconds later, Firefox ran out of the tent while she held a white envelope. She dashed straight for the trees.

Firefox's face, except for twin smears of pie-goop on each side of her face, was clean.

I thought unladylike words. I was just as mad at myself as I was at Firefox—*I* should have thought up that trick!

Through the tent flap, I could see a long table that was covered with a white tablecloth. That table was heavily laden with food—but it was not the food that interested me.

At the front of the table was a white envelope, propped up and marked *11*; next to the white envelope were two small drawstring bags, which were marked *2* and *12*.

I saw all this in an instant, while I was running full speed toward the tent flap.

Move it, move it, hurry!

"Yoo-hoo!" I heard Garlic's voice say.

Without thinking, I turned my face to the left.

Garlic had already thrown a pie; it was headed straight for my face.

I twisted my upper body to face Garlic directly, then my left hand knocked Garlic's pie away. I grinned at my enemy.

Meanwhile, I had pulled out a pie of my own. I threw it at Garlic.

Then I resumed running for the tent.

Garlic leaned sideways, plus my aim was off, so—*splat!*—the pie hit her shoulder instead of her face.

Garlic stuck her tongue out at me. I almost did not notice this, because of the red-metallic things crawling on her face.

Soon I was at the white-tablecloth table, so I had other things on my mind besides Garlic and her cooties.

"Wow, Supreme pizza!" said a male voice from inches away. "Potato chips! Chocolate cake!"

I spun around. Standing next to me was Cakedough!

I jammed my hand into my open pie-carry bag, with plans to pie Cakedough's face, when he held up a hand—

"Truce. If you won't pie us right now, we won't pie you till we're done eating."

"*Move*, Cakedough!" Garlic yelled. "I can't pie Fire Bitch with you in the way."

I looked at Cakedough and said, " 'We'? Garlic doesn't want to make this deal."

Cakedough rolled his eyes. "Not her! *We* means the voices in our head."

"Uh, sure, it's a deal," I said. "You guys enjoy the food."

Cakedough said, "Lucky for you, only four voices in our head want to pie you this instant. They're outvoted."

Then Cakedough grinned, and yelled at Garlic, "Check this out! They have corny dogs here, and macaroni and cheese, *and* spinach-and-liver casserole. *Yummy!*"

I thought, *You do realize, I trust, that the spinach-and-liver casserole is left over from yesterday?* Meanwhile, I had grabbed up Twelve's little gift bag, and was slipping the drawstrings around my left wrist.

"Move out of the frigging way, Cakedough, if you won't pie Fire Bitch yourself," yelled Garlic. "*Jeez!*"

Garlic threw a pie at me, even though she did not have a clear shot. Most of the pie hit Cakedough's shoulder, but some pie-goop went right in my eyes.

Splat, instant blindness.

By then I had a pie in my hand. I threw it at where I thought Garlic was. No surprise, I missed.

I had just wiped pie-goop out of my eyes when someone grabbed my left hand, and I was swung to the ground.

****

I wound up lying on the grass on my right side, my right hand pinned under me, and my pie-carry bag lying on the grass just in front of me. Garlic quickly straddled my upthrust left hip.

I tried to roll Garlic off me, but achieved nothing—she was way too heavy. I glared at her, not showing my despair. *This is it.*

Garlic had a pie in her hand, so I was confused when she laid the pie on the grass instead of pieing me.

Garlic reached inside her apron and pulled out a bottle of Acme Chloroform. "Look what Cakedough and I found in one of our walks through the woods. We found a little green building, and inside was this stuff. It'll knock you out if you breathe it. *Beg* me not to knock you out now."

Garlic put one hand on the cap of the bottle, but did not yet unscrew that cap.

I said, "The shed is blue, not green. It used to have a bunch of pies in it too, but I accidentally threw them all face-down on the ground. Whoops."

Garlic glared at me, then she twisted the cap off the chloroform bottle.

I was shoved onto my back, then I felt something wet hit my throat. Garlic rolled me back onto my side and resumed straddling my hip, while I smelled chloroform fumes.

Garlic grinned down at me. "I just dumped a ton of chloroform on your t-shirt. Feeling dizzy yet? Soon you'll pass out, and it will be frigging easy for me to pie you."

Even as I was feeling woozy, I tried again to roll Garlic off. No cigar.

Garlic grinned. "And even if you get away from me, you'll pass out from the fumes and then somebody will pie you. You can't win, Fire Bitch."

"I *will* win," I said. "I promised my sister and Flew."

Garlic laughed. "You promised Flew, your pathetic little ally, that you'd *win?* Not gonna happen. We Gluttons pieed *her*, and in a minute, I'm going to pie *you*. And then poor Loverboy won't get his medicine, *aww*."

I didn't reply with words; instead, I rolled onto my back enough that I managed to spit in Garlic's face.

"Change of plans, *bitch*," Garlic murmured, as she shoved the open bottle of chloroform under my nose. "I'm going to *kill* you now, and make it look—"

Suddenly all of Garlic's weight on me vanished. I was free to move.

****

"—asking you a question, girl: What you do to Flew?" a male voice was yelling. "You pie that little girl?"

When I stood up, I saw three things that were new.

Garlic's chloroform bottle was lying in the grass, a few feet from where she had set down her pie; and the red cap to the chloroform bottle was lying in the grass.

The biggest new thing to happen was that Thrash was here and he was yelling at Garlic. Thrash was holding Garlic by her shoulders, a foot off the ground.

Up this close, he looks as big as a mountain.

"No, I didn't pie her!" Garlic said. "I swear, it wasn't me! *Cakedough!*"

"Hold on," Cakedough replied, "we're still eating." Cakedough did not even turn to look.

"You know her name," Thrash said to Garlic. "How you know her name if you ain't pieed Flew like you gonna pie this girl here?"

Thrash didn't give Garlic a chance to answer. One hand moved to press Garlic against his chest, while his other hand grabbed the back of Garlic's head. Thrash hurried over to the Corny Dog, then the powerful hand that was holding the back of Garlic's head, rushed forward and down.

Garlic's face got shoved into a pie that was laying atop the Corny Dog.

Splat!

"Yeere *out!*" a referee declared.

Thrash let Garlic drop to the ground. Thrash turned to face me.

I gulped. *I should have run when I had the chance.*

****

Thrash said to me, "What she mean? About Flew be you ally?"

"I— I—we teamed up. We skunked up the supplies. I tried to save her, I did. But he got there first. School Zone One."

"And you pieed him?"

"Yes, I pieed him. And I tried to lay flowers all around her. I *did* sing her to sleep."

Thrash looked confused. "To sleep?"

"To unconsciousness. I sang until she passed out. Eleven, they sent me beef jerky. . . . Pie me fast, okay, Thrash?"

Thrash's eyes got thoughtful for a time, then he shook his head. "Just this one time, I let you go. For Flew. You and me, we even then. No more owed. You understand?"

I nodded, not trusting myself to speak.

Thrash said no more to me. He ran to the tent, and got right next to still-feasting Cakedough. Thrash grabbed the white envelope off the white table—

"Hey, watch it!" Cakedough said. Then he noticed who his new neighbor was. "WHAT THE HECK?"

—Thrash grabbed Eleven's white envelope, *then* he grabbed Two's drawstring bag, then he ran for the trees.

I, meanwhile, had bent down to pick up the bottle of chloroform and its red cap. I screwed the cap on the bottle, and shoved the bottle in my apron, so that nobody else could use the chloroform against me again.

With all that done, I ran for the trees myself.

Or I tried to. Garlic had been correct: The chloroform fumes coming from my t-shirt were making me woozy.

"GARLIC? OH GOD, *GARLIC!*" I heard Cakedough yell behind me.

That's when "Pachelbel's Canon" and Barnacle Brained's announcement made Garlic's elimination official.

"COME BACK HERE, BIG BOY!" Cakedough yelled. "WE WILL DESTROY YOU!" Heavy footsteps ran in a different direction than toward me.

****

Those chloroform fumes were really trashing my brain. I was staggering by the time I made my way back to the red maintenance shed and through the door.

Poofa was still unconscious.

It took me several minutes, but I managed to remove the little drawstring bag and the pie-carry bag, and managed to put those bags on the worktable.

Inside the drawstring bag were two long, thin boxes:

• Acme Labs BALLZ-FIXER 3000™
• Acme Labs COOTIES-B-GONE 3000™

I opened each box. Inside was what looked like a ball-point pen with a half-inch needle at the tip.

My vision was starting to blur by then, so reading the instructions was out of the question. I jammed each "pen" into one of Poofa's biceps, and hoped this was good enough.

I stuck Poofa twice, then I passed out.

Chapter 20
Kissing And
Kindergarten

"Uhh," I said, when my eyes next opened. I was usually a better conversationalist than this.

The first thing I noticed was that I was lying on my back and staring at an unfinished ceiling. Something light was laying on my chest, and my throat and upper chest were wet. In fact, water was running off me.

Poofa was standing by the worktable, looking down at my face. "Karen, are you all right? Are you okay?"

Is Poofa still ravaged by cooties? "I'm fine," I said, "but how are *you?*"

Poofa *seemed to be* back to normal: tall, strong, and blond. But was he *really* okay?

"I'm feeling good, actually," he replied. "I have only a twinge of pain when I walk around, and the pain is fading. As for the cooties, I woke up surrounded by a boatload of dead bugs. So I used the garden hose to wash 'em out the door."

"Garden hose?" I said. I put my hand on the thing laying on my chest, and felt a cylindrical rubber shape. "Why is the garden hose laying on me and pouring water on me?"

"Because I had to get the chloroform out of your t-shirt somehow. If it were *my* t-shirt, I'd just take the shirt off, hang it over a tree branch, and blast the shirt with the hose till the shirt didn't smell funny anymore. But then I realized you wouldn't like waking up bare-chested."

"I wouldn't be bare-chested, because I'm wearing a bra."

"*Ahem*, I know. The wet t-shirt is clinging to it."

Poofa was already blushing—and with that last remark, I started blushing too.

I said, "Would you take the hose outside, then? And then *stay* outside till I know I'm decent?"

"Oh, Karen, you're much more than decent," Poofa said. He walked over, picked up the end of the hose, and walked out the open door of the maintenance shed.

I discovered that I was not wearing my apron. I then discovered that my apron, my pie-carry bag, and Garlic's bottle of chloroform were waiting for me on the worktable.

I realized that yes, my t-shirt was now wet and clingy; but if I put on my apron and my pie-carry bag over my wet t-shirt, the crazed lechers would *probably* bother someone else. So this was what I did.

The bottle of chloroform, I left on the worktable.

I walked outside. Just to the right of the door, a hoe and a steel rake were leaning against the wall of the shed. They had been there the entire time that I had been at the maintenance shed; I just had not noticed them till now.

I found Poofa on the window-side of the maintenance shed, coiling the garden hose that was connected to an outdoor faucet.

Poofa looked great—no longer short, flabby, or nerdy. It warmed . . . my pride . . . to see that my risky plan to get him medicine had succeeded so well.

Poofa looked at me when I walked up to him. He smiled. "This place is beautiful, and it just got *more* beautiful."

"Um," I said, blushing anew, "your zits are gone. And your voice sounds like it used to."

"I have *you* to thank for all that," Poofa said.

Poofa leaned down to kiss me, I tilted my head up to kiss him, inhaling his baked-bread scent—

This was when the downpour began.

****

Seconds later, Poofa looked out through the doorway at the pouring rain. "I feel sorry for those four miserable contestants stuck out there."

"Three contestants. Garlic got pieed."

"By you?"

"By Thrash."

"Lucky for you, he didn't pie you too."

"He was going to, till he found out about me and Flew. Then he let me go."

"He *what?*"

So as the rain rained, I told Poofa everything that had happened after I had daisy-tricked him—

But for Poofa to understand what the big deal with Thrash was, I had to go back further. I told Poofa about my alliance with Flew; and Flew's and my trick that we pulled on the Gluttons, so that I could skunk their goodies; and Marblecake pieing Flew; and me pieing Marblecake, then singing Flew to sleep; then School Zone Eleven sending me a gift of beef jerky.

Poofa said, "I *love* beef jerky. That was a real nice gift they sent you."

"*It wasn't a gift!* It was *payback*—or rather, as much payback as Eleven could manage. When Thrash let me go, that was more payback."

" 'Payback.' What an unkind reason to act kind to someone."

I felt frustrated; why couldn't he see? "It's just like you and me and that wedding cake—I could give you a million dollars *after* curing your cooties, but that wouldn't make up for you saving my life, *and* Primmy's life, *and* Mom's life, back when you and I were eleven."

He sighed. "I guess I don't understand. Mainly because I didn't give you that wedding cake *when you were starving* so I could get a big payback later."

I sighed. "I agree, you don't understand."

I looked outside, at the still-pouring rain. I normally loved to argue, with everyone but Primmy. But now I wanted my arguing with Poofa to stop. So I changed the subject—

"I think we would like Thrash. I think he'd be our friend back in School Zone Twelve."

"Then let's hope Cakedough pies him, so we don't have to."

****

After a minute of watching the rain pour down, I turned back to face Poofa. (And to face the ESPN camera that was watching through the knothole, though I pretended to be unaware of that.)

I realized I did not want to lose the kid with the cake. Not to Cakedough; not to Thrash; not to the sneaky redhead. I wanted to keep Poofa next to me till the end of the Dessert Games, but *not* for the glory of School Zone Twelve.

I looked at Poofa, intending to say such things, but then Poofa walked over to me. His blue eyes got closer to my gray eyes as he bent down.

"I just remembered," he said, "I was about to thank you for curing my ills, when the rain hit." He kissed me.

I liked the kiss—it was the first kiss that we were both fully aware of. Neither of us hobbled by sickness or pain, or simply unconscious. This was the first kiss where I actually felt stirring inside my chest. This was the first kiss that made me want another kiss.

I did not get another kiss. "We should leave here soon," Poofa said. "Even if this means going out in the rain."

I took this to mean that we were leaving now. I started to move toward the worktable.

"We don't need to leave *yet*," he said. He did not kiss me then, but he *did* put his arms around me.

Again I felt good feelings—I felt *safe*.

No one had held me like this in such a long time. Since my father had died and I had stopped trusting my mother, no one else's arms made me feel this safe.

To make this good moment last longer, I said, "Poofa, you said at the interview, you'd had a crush on me 'forever.' When did 'forever' start?"

Poofa shocked me then, by talking about our first day of kindergarten. Mr. Meadowlark had pointed little-me out to little-boy Poofa—

****

Mr. Meadowlark bent down and murmured to his five-year-old son, "See that little girl there? I wanted to marry her mother, but instead, Blanche married a man named Phillip."

"Why did she marry *him* and not *you?*"

"Because when he sings, all the animals nearby sing along. Well, *that* plus I'm actually more attracted to abusive women than to nice women, so I didn't fight to keep her."

Little Poofa didn't know what to think. His father, unlike his mother and older brothers, never lied to him. But what Dad had just told him sure sounded like a whopper.

That afternoon, little Poofa found out the truth of his father's words. The music teacher asked if anyone knew "The Star-Spangled Banner." Little Karen's hand shot up.

Little Karen not only knew the first verse, and sang it all on key—a nearly-impossible task—but when she started singing the second verse, birds flew in the open windows and provided background vocals.

By Karen's fourth verse of "The Star-Spangled Banner," birds, cats, and dogs were in the classroom, singing along with Karen. A black bear had appeared from nowhere and was outside under the open kindergarten windows, singing the bass harmony.

****

". . . So there you stood, Karen, singing your heart out. I'll never forget you in your twin black braids, wearing a t-shirt that showed a smiling, bright-red puppy."

I blinked in surprise.

I did not remember wearing the "Clifford's Puppy Days" t-shirt on that first day of school, but I *did* own it back then. Heck, Primmy wore the t-shirt after I had outgrown it, till it faded in the wash.

Likewise, I did not remember what song I had sung that first day, but I did remember that one of the animals that had sung along with me had been a purple poodle. *Who on Earth dyes a poodle purple?*

I could not avoid the conclusion: Poofa did indeed remember our first day of kindergarten, eleven years later!

"Whoa," I said. "You have a remarkable memory. I am impressed."

Poofa shrugged. "A good memory and a dollar will get me a cup of coffee."

I said, "I don't have a dollar in my pocket. Will you settle for a kiss?"

I was still kissing Poofa when the silver drone helicopter landed just outside the door.

It was Poofa who braved the rain to claim our gifts from Sumbitch.

Poofa got two replacement lemon-meringue pies. I got two replacement pies of a different filling. And as reward for the two of us baring our souls on ESPN, we received—

—one bag of trail mix, to split two ways.

Bleep.

Poofa said, "Too bad our little show isn't going out on Lifetime instead of ESPN."

"I don't take cable, remember?"

"Um, what I mean is: If our romantic conversation had aired on Lifetime, we would have received *at least* a picnic basket. With lamb stew included for sure."

I grinned—till I imagined Soozin frowning at me. *"Maybe half a bag of trail mix is all you deserve, heartbreaker."*

Chapter 21
Firefox Outfoxed Us

Included with the bag of trail mix—that Poofa and I were supposed to split—were two white-plastic spoons and two paper plates. I was sure that the spoons and plates were Bimbie Bauble's doing. Even when eating trail mix, a person must show proper table manners!

I said to Poofa, "You talked about leaving this shed and finding the other contestants. But it seems to me that as long as we're eating, it's okay to stay inside this dry building."

Poofa nodded. "Makes sense."

I set out the paper plates, opened up the trail-mix bag, reached in with my clean plastic spoon, and gave Poofa and me each—four teaspoons.

I was in *no* hurry to eat this stuff up. Because then we would have to go out in the rain.

****

It was while Poofa was spooning out more trail mix for us that our mood was suddenly saddened—

"Pachelbel's Canon" played. "Attention, contestants," Barnacle Brained announced, "Thrash Okeniyi of School Zone Eleven has been eliminated. Four contestants remain."

I turned my face away from the knothole (and away from the camera that was watching Poofa and me through the knothole). I muttered, "What a bummer."

As soon as I said that, the downpour began to ease off. Within three minutes, the only water coming down was what dripped from the trees.

During those three minutes, I stared out the open door, while I spoke no words but I thought many words.

Soon Poofa and I will leave the maintenance shed. Soon we will find Cakedough and Firefox, or they will find us. Soon the Dessert Games will end.

If Poofa and I both win, will we still be friends? Or will we be more than friends?

If one of us loses, will we still be friends?

Do I want Poofa to be my boyfriend? Or only a friend? Or do I want to never see him again?

Do I want a boy who wears more makeup than I do, to be my boyfriend?

What will Soozin think about Poofa and me being friends of some kind? How much do I care what Soozin thinks?

****

After the rain stopped, Poofa and I kissed in celebration. Then we finished off the trail mix.

I decided that kissing made trail mix taste better—*and kissing is low in calories!*

****

Out of the corner of my eye, I thought I saw the maintenance shed's little window get darker for a second.

But when I turned my head to look out the glass, everything was fine.

Still, I decided to check. Sort of—

• I rushed out the door of the maintenance shed.

• I turned right and hurried to the corner of the shed.

• In so doing, my elbow knocked over the rake that leaned against the wall by the door. I did not stop to pick up the rake, even though its prongs were pointing straight up and this could hurt someone.

• I peeked around the corner of the shed to the window-side of the shed. I saw nobody.

• I turned around, stepped over the fallen rake, hurried past the open door, and peeked around the other long wall of the shed. Again I saw nobody.

• I rushed to the end of the windowless long wall and looked around the corner. I saw that our "Peeping Tom" ESPN camera was still looking through the knothole, but no person was there.

I guess I was imagining things.

Walking back to the door of the maintenance shed, I spotted a second red ESPN camera, about twenty yards away. It rotated leftward to keep me in view until I went inside.

Once I was inside, Poofa asked me why I had suddenly dashed outside. I told him why, casually mentioning the second ESPN camera as I explained.

Poofa replied, "If the camera operators are getting bored, the referees might be getting bored too. We should leave now, before the referees come in and drag us out. Or worse yet, the referees might eliminate us on the spot."

"They can't do that!"

"Are you *sure* about that? Absolutely *sure?* We've been sitting out the contest for a long, long time—maybe the refs will penalize us for that."

I was *not* sure. So with a sigh, I agreed to pack up and move out. Our first stop: to go outside to the garden hose and to refill our water bottles.

Once Poofa had the end of the hose in his left hand, he held out his right hand. "Give me your water bottle and I'll refill it."

"*No!*" I said, smiling. "I can fill my own bottle, thank you. Besides, if you fill my bottle, I'll owe you."

"Pay me with a kiss?"

"We're supposed to be *moving*, remember?"

"Then how about some beef jerky? I can eat that as we walk."

"Fine, but, *ahem*, you'll have to open it first."

"Not a problem. I'm big and strong, remember?"

I turned around and rushed back around the corner, and I stepped over the rake. My footsteps near the wall of the shed made a strange echo that I had not noticed before: The echo sounded like a second set of footsteps.

I hurried in the door, then walked over to my backpack. Seconds later, I was outside again, hurrying toward Poofa with my gift-package of beef jerky.

The packaging that I had not been able to open at all, took Poofa barely over an instant to open. *Grr.*

Poofa took out a jerky-stick, bit off one end, and chewed. "*Mmm*, delicious."

Then he looked past me and said, "I wonder what all that is about?"

Referees, a golf cart, and a third red ESPN camera had appeared from nowhere, and were all moving toward us.

****

I thought at first that all these people were looking at Poofa and me.

Even as the referees broke into a run, this was what I thought.

But then, when the referees and the golf-cart driver came close, I noticed that they were not looking at us, but were looking to the right of us.

They were looking at the shed's door!

"Poofa," I said, "I think someone is in the shed."

After all, why else would two more TV cameras show up, unless another contestant was nearby?

Then I flipped that logic around—

"Poofa, if another contestant got close to the shed, he'd see the camera peering through the knothole and he'd know that someone was in the shed."

Poofa said, "And now he knows we're out of the shed. We need to get our pies!"

Poofa dropped the water hose and we broke into a run.

When we rounded the corner of the maintenance shed, so that we could see the shed's open door and the prongs of the fallen rake, we found out we were too late.

But *Cakedough* was not who had gotten the drop on us.

Firefox had just stepped out the door. She was wearing my pie-carry bag, and she was holding one of Sumbitch's new gift-pies in each hand.

When she first saw us, she looked panicked for an instant. Then her face shifted into a sly smile.

Meanwhile, Poofa and I had stopped running. We looked at Firefox; she looked at us. Silence followed, except for the running feet and the panting of referees.

Firefox nodded at the bag of beef jerky that Poofa was holding. "Unless beef jerky is allowed now as an eliminator, you two can't fight back. Even better, I'm standing between you and all your pies."

She smiled and added, "After you two, I'll face Cakedough. He's slow, I'm sure. Then I can eat all the strawberry shortcake I want, *myuhaha!*"

Poofa stepped forward, clearly intending to shield my body with his. He said, "Don't worry, Karen, I'll save you."

It's a good thing that rolling eyes do not make a sound, or Poofa's pride would have been *so* crushed.

Meanwhile, Poofa was saying, "If you're going to pie someone, Firefox, pie *me*."

Firefox smiled. "Suit yourself."

Still smiling, Firefox strutted toward Poofa and me.

I yelled, "Run around her! Get in the shed—"

Poofa said, "I'm not leav—"

Firefox stepped on the prongs of the rake. The handle of the rake spun a quarter-turn—*FWAP!*—smacking Firefox's face and the front of her body all at once. *Hard.*

Firefox fell back, slightly off balance. Maybe if her hands had been empty, she could have regained her balance; or at worse, she might have broken her fall with her hands.

But instead, Firefox's butt, shoulders, and head all slammed against the ground. The two pies flew up in the air.

One pie fell on the grass.

The other pie landed—*splat!*—squarely on Firefox's face.

A red-faced, panting referee ruled, "The School Zone Five female has been eliminated."

Firefox tried to sit up. "No. That . . . isn't . . ." Then her eyes closed and she fell back.

I looked at the pie-goop on her face. "What kind of filling is that? It isn't lemon meringue."

Less than a minute later, Poofa reported back, "Firefox was taken out by boysenberry."

Chapter 22
Poofa Made A Friend

Seconds later, we heard Barnacle Brained: "Attention, contestants. Firefox Emerson of School Zone Five has been eliminated. Three contestants remain."

So now Cakedough knew it was time for the showdown.

Brained's announcement came as I was explaining to Poofa why Firefox sneaking into the red maintenance shed had not been wild bad luck—

"... how she knew about the tripwire. Watching patiently was also how she knew *we* had been in the shed, and how she knew when we *left*. When she walked in, she got lucky, finding all those pies."

Poofa said, "But then she got *un*lucky, stepping on that rake."

Poofa walked over, picked up the rake, and let it fall against his shoulder like a rifle. "I'm taking the rake with us. Maybe we can use it on Cakedough."

"Huh? How can a rake help us beat Cakedough?"

Poofa smiled, clearly proud of himself. "I drop the rake down in front of him if he's chasing after us, prongs up, and maybe he'll pie himself like Firefox did."

I'm glad I never think up ideas this stupid. I figured that the odds of Cakedough pieing himself the same way that Firefox had done, were millions to one.

But I did not tell Poofa that his idea was silly. Instead, I kissed him on the mouth—gotta play to those sponsors, remember—and I said, "You're so clever."

Poofa's smile beamed.

Actually, I did not kiss Poofa only to hype our "romance"—it turned out, he was actually fun to kiss. But this did not mean I was falling in love, nosirree.

****

We have to hurry! We have to get moving <u>now!</u>

When I had taken back my pie-carry bag from passed-out Firefox, I had discovered that the bag had been a gooey, yucchy mess inside. It took me fifteen minutes with the garden hose to clean out the insides of the pie-carry bag.

And who knew what Cakedough was doing, or where he was going, during those fifteen minutes?

It took Poofa and me only five more minutes to leave the shed for good. I walked away from the shed with the pie-carry bag clean and loaded with three pies. I carried Flew's police whistle in my apron pocket, and I had Garlic's bottle of chloroform tucked behind my apron.

I was wearing three pies that were strapped to me, and I was carrying a fourth pie, in case Cakedough surprised us.

Poofa walked beside me, wearing my backpack (which was empty, except for the leafy poncho, water bottles, and his beloved beef jerky). Poofa's right hand carried a pie; his left hand carried the rake on his shoulder.

We walked among the trees, looking for Cakedough. I asked Poofa to loudly sing "Ninety-Nine Bottles Of Beer." Poofa frowned, and he looked like he would refuse to sing it. But then he sang.

Ninety-nine bottles of beer on the wall,
Ninety-nine bottles of beer.
Take one down, and pass it around,
Ninety-eight bottles of beer on the wall.

The birds did not sing along with Poofa, which I thought was strange. After all, birds always sang along with *me* when *I* sang. Had the birds suddenly turned sick?

While Poofa sang loudly and walked, I walked and kept the beat with the police whistle. The vampires (zombies?) in School Zone Thirteen surely could hear us, we were that loud. But either Cakedough was deaf, or he was hiding from us.

****

Where is he?

Poofa and I walked and walked, and we made music loudly. We saw no sign of Cakedough.

The sun was low in the western sky now; I was sure that the Piemakers wanted to wrap this up by sunset. If Poofa and I did not find Cakedough soon or he did not find us soon, the Piemakers would force the three of us together.

I was sure I would not enjoy the Piemakers' meddling.

Cakedough, where are you? And what will you be up to when we find you?

****

As our walking and singing took us near the big fountain, I warned Poofa about the troll under one of the bridges. What I *thought* would happen next was that Poofa would take care to avoid a surprise attack by the troll.

Instead, Poofa responded with "I want to meet him."

"You didn't hear me. He's a *troll*."

"I heard you. Look, you wouldn't have found me without his help. Because you found me, I'm now cured of my cooties. So I *owe* him. Weren't you trying to explain *owing* to me?"

"*Fine*. The troll you think you owe something to, is under this little bridge we're about to walk across."

Poofa did not walk over the bridge. Instead, he turned right and walked along the near bank of the concrete trough that went under the bridge. Then Poofa quickly turned around and squatted down.

"Hello, Mr. Troll," Poofa said.

"*What?*" the troll exclaimed. "How did you know I was—oh, you're with *her*."

Poofa said cheerfully, "Anyway, I want to thank you for helping Karen find me. My name—"

"Hold on. You want to *thank* me, human boy?"

Poofa smiled at me. "Yeah, because lots of good things happened after Karen found me."

Poofa turned his attention back to the troll. "So, my name is Poofa; what's *your* name?"

"I don't have a name. No troll has a name."

"Why not?" Poofa asked, surprised.

I interrupted: "Because nobody wants to talk to a troll if she can avoid it." I stared the troll down.

The troll shrugged. "Like she said."

Poofa said, "But *I* want to talk to you. I can't just say *Hey, troll*—that isn't nice. Is it okay if I call you *Trent*?"

"You're giving me a *name*, Poofa?"

"Even better, I'm trying to give you a *strong* name. Is *Trent* okay? Do you like it?"

"I. . ." The troll was blinking rapidly. "I seem to have something in my eye."

"*Both* eyes," I said. "*Both* eyes are—"

Besides the troll now having two shiny eyes, he also was smiling—yes, a smile was shining on that ugly, dirty face.

The smiling troll said, "What can I do for you, Poofa? I'm sorry I can't offer you any toddler sandwiches; I'm all out. Can I help you with anything else?"

I said, "Poofa, we *really* need to get going now."

"Hold on, Karen."

Poofa said to the troll, "Trent, Karen and I are looking for a boy. He's blond-haired like me, and really fat. Have you seen him?"

"Is he an *old* boy? Seventeen or eighteen?"

"Yes! You've seen him?"

"Yes, Poofa. I don't mess with boys that old—they're not tasty." The troll did not seem to be joking.

The troll pointed. "The fat blond boy went that way. Toward the fake lake."

Poofa rushed forward and gave the troll's hand fifteen seconds of mighty shaking. "Thank you so much, Trent."

A tear, which was bright with reflected light, ran down the troll's cheek. "No, thank *you*."

Then the troll added, "Poofa, please, one thing before you go?"

"Hm?"

The troll said, "When movie adaptations of a book are very different from that book, it's always because greedy Hollywood types disrespect the author."

****

Poofa stopped singing "Ninety-Nine Bottles Of Beer" when we got near to the blue maintenance shed. That was when we realized we had a problem: What if Cakedough were hiding in that shed?

"That's easy," Poofa said. "I'll check inside by myself. If Cakedough pies me, then you pie him for the win."

"Nuh-uh," I answered. "I want us *both* to win."

"Karen, I don't care if I win or not, so long as *you* do. Now *stay back* and cover me."

Poofa walked forward, with the rake still at his shoulder. He walked past the golf cart that was parked by the blue shed's door. I stayed back like he had asked me to, about five yards behind the golf cart. *But* I had a pie in hand, ready to throw it if Cakedough appeared.

Poofa opened the door of the blue shed, walked in, and walked out two seconds later with a bottle of Acme Chloroform in his hand. Poofa's face had not been pieed.

When Poofa returned to me, he said, "There are lots of pies splattered in the grass, but there are no pies inside. I *did* find this, however." Poofa held the bottle of chloroform out to me. "Here, take it."

I said, "I already have *one* bottle of chloroform. Why do I need *two?*"

Still, I took the offered bottle and stuck it behind my apron, to keep its twin from getting lonely.

Meanwhile, Poofa was frowning at me. "Why give it to *you? Because you* have proven you're willing to use chloroform on people, to get what you want."

Since that was true, I did not argue the point. I said only, "Let's continue to the lake, okay?"

****

While we were walking, Poofa asked me, "Why do you think Cakedough and Garlic hate you so much?"

I said, "Three reasons. First, those two are supposed to be special because they volunteered for this, right? Though I have to say, it sure seems fishy how six kids in three school zones got their names Selected, then *all six kids* declared themselves 'unfit' so that the Gluttons could volunteer. Anyway, instead of six volunteers this year, I make seven, so being a volunteer isn't as special."

Poofa replied, "Yeah, that makes sense."

"Second, before the gong sounded, the Gluttons were making fun of all the non-Glutton kids, remember? 'We're going to win, and you have no chance.' But then *I* started dissing *the Gluttons*. Turns out, Cakedough and Garlic can dish it out, but they don't like taking it."

"And the third reason those two hate you?"

"Maybe because I'm slim, while Cakedough and Garlic are each a tub of lard?"

****

By the time Poofa and I reached the fake lake, only six bottles of beer were left on the wall. We saw no sign that Cakedough was at the fake lake.

Poofa and I walked around the shore of the fake lake till we were standing on the Corny Dog's meadow. We then walked around the meadow, looking for Cakedough.

The gold-painted Corny Dog no longer glowed, because late-evening shadows shaded the entire Corny Dog.

We saw plenty of referees in the meadow, we saw plenty of red ESPN cameras, and we saw four golf carts with bored-looking drivers—but we saw no sign of Cakedough. He was not anywhere in the meadow, and he was not hiding in the trees by the edges of the meadow.

Poofa and I walked to the end of the meadow that doubled as shore for the fake lake. I sat down and said, "I'm not walking another step. When Cakedough wants to end this, *he* can come find *me*."

Poofa sat down next to me. "Sounds like a plan."

I said, "Where *is* Cakedough? Doesn't he know that this is the day it *ends?*"

"Um, Karen? This is also the day it *starts*. Remember, the Selection was this morning."

"I'm bored now. I feel like singing."

Poofa smiled. "You know that I love to hear you sing. But I can't sing along—all those bottles of beer have made my throat hurt."

I smiled at him. "Let the birds sing with me if they want."

I began to sing the song I had sung to Flew: "*Thick, sizzle-ling steak. . .*"

The birds in the trees did not sing words, but they tweeted the melody line for "*Cut with steak knife agleam. . .*"

I sang, "*With it, big taters. . .*"

Bird-tweets answered: "*Filled with tart sour cream. . .*"

I finished the first verse: "*Where you are going, the food tastes so good.*"

I was just taking a breath to sing the second verse when the birds in the trees *screamed.*

The birds stopped tweeting along with me; they began to tweet a different song, but one I recognized. Its lyrics were—

Goodbye—we're out of sun,
Goodbye—it's time to run,
Goodbye—we had such fun,
Goodbye, we're gone, goodbye!

I thought, *Something is wrong.*

By now, both Poofa and I were standing up, and I was ready to throw the pie I had been carrying.

Cakedough rushed out from the trees then, running full speed. That *cheater* was wearing the wire-mesh fencing mask that I had seen by the blue maintenance shed. With that mask on, I could not pie Cakedough's face!

I threw the pie anyway. *Splat!* It should have counted—if Cakedough had not been wearing that stupid mask, I would have hit him right in the face. But all I achieved was to blind Cakedough for a tiny instant.

Even blinded, Cakedough was still running. He ran a hand over the wire mesh of his fencing mask, enabling him to see, then he kept running toward Poofa and me—

—He ran *past* us. Cakedough then made a right turn, now rushing straight for the Corny Dog.

What is Cakedough doing? I wondered. *What is he up to?*

Then seven clowns ran out of the trees, from where Cakedough had come. Those clowns started running along the shore toward Poofa and me.

I suspected *strongly* that these were not clowns who would make balloon animals, or who would pull silly stunts to make me laugh.

"RUN, KAREN!" Poofa yelled.

I ran straight for the Corny Dog.

Chapter 23
Cakedough And Clowns

The clowns wore enormous red shoes, and neck-to-ankle long-sleeved white costumes with enormous blue fake buttons going down the front. The clowns wore starched white collars that stuck straight out from their necks.

The clowns wore the expected clown makeup—a whited-out face with whited-out eyebrows, drawn-in eyebrows and a drawn-in smiling mouth—except for one strange thing. The clowns' red noses were their real noses, painted red, instead of round, red, fake noses.

All the clowns, whether male or female, were wearing some kind of flat hat on their heads.

This was all I had time to notice before I ran straight for the Corny Dog.

****

"Oof! *Nuts*," I heard Poofa say.

I looked back. Poofa had tripped over a tree root and had fallen down. Thank heavens, he was no longer carrying that silly rake. Alas, his pie was splattered on the ground.

When Poofa saw me looking at him, he said, "*Run*, Karen! I'll catch up." Even as he spoke, he was standing up again.

I did as Poofa told me—I ran.

But when I reached the stick of the Corny Dog, climbed atop the Corny Dog, and looked back, I saw that Poofa was fifteen yards away.

Walking with a limp.

And the clowns were coming closer.

I heard music then: the song "It's A Happy, Happy Day." The song was coming from an ice-cream truck that was racing along the shore of the fake lake. Once the ice-cream truck came alongside the meadow, the truck turned right and zoomed toward the Corny Dog. When the ice-cream truck came near the Corny Dog, brakes screeched. The truck made a quick half-turn, then stopped so that the back of the truck faced the Corny Dog.

Two clowns yanked open the back of the ice-cream truck. Inside were pies, which the two clowns quickly handed out to other clowns.

Soon, every clown was holding a pie in each hand. Lucky for Poofa and me, no clowns were throwing their pies yet.

I looked over at Cakedough, who now was sitting atop the Corny Dog. Cakedough was panting and his clothes were sweaty—at the moment, Cakedough was no threat.

Whoosh. While I had been looking at Cakedough, some clown had thrown a pie but had missed.

I looked back at Poofa and to the clowns surrounding him—

I saw about twenty clowns now, with an equal mix of men and women. The clowns had pulled their flat hats down over their clown-faces; those "hats" turned out to be each a cardboard photo of a kid's face.

By now, I was standing astride the long pie-shelf that ran along the top of the Corny Dog. Even though my pie-carry bag held three pies in it, I immediately bent down and grabbed two pies from the Corny Dog shelf.

Whoosh. A man-clown threw a pie at Poofa, but Poofa leaned to the side and the pie missed.

I threw one pie at that clown. I hit him in the face.

Or rather, I pieed the clown's photo-mask.

The clown did not faint. He did not even wobble.

That cardboard mask is shielding that clown from chloroform fumes in the pie-filling.

I yelled down, "Poofa, climb on top of the Corny Dog!"

Poofa yelled back, "I'm trying. My ankle hurts."

If *a pie* would not take that clown out, *chloroform* would. I reached into my apron, yanked out Garlic's mostly-full bottle of chloroform, unscrewed the cap, and splashed knock-out chemical on the clown's cardboard face.

Down he went. He stayed down.

A woman-clown brought her arm back, clearly intending to pie Poofa. Her face got chloroform-splashed too.

The clowns were distracted for a moment, as they looked down at their passed-out comrades. That was when Poofa broke away and hobbled toward the gold-painted stick of the Corny Dog.

I glanced over at Cakedough. He was sitting in the same place and was still panting. He was not a problem yet.

I thought, *Now is the best time in the world to pie Cakedough.*

Just when I was about to run over and pie Cakedough, I saw that Poofa was having trouble climbing up onto the stick of the Corny Dog.

So instead of finishing Cakedough off, I ran toward the stick to help Poofa.

Splat! Poofa's shoulder got pieed. *You missed, clown!*

As soon as I could grab any part of Poofa, I grabbed him and pulled up.

A woman-clown grabbed Poofa and tried to pull him down.

This is when I noticed that the clown's cardboard-photo face was not just *anyone's* face, it was *Glandular's* face!

Next I noticed that the top blue fake-button on her clown-suit had a *1* in the middle of the blue.

I shrieked in horror. "The clown, she's Glandular!"

With my free hand, I rushed to splash chloroform on the Glandular-clown's cardboard face. Down she went.

I glanced around at the other clowns. A woman-clown whose top button said *11* was wearing Flew's face. A man-clown whose top button said *11* was wearing Thrash's face. I quickly spotted the faces of Marblecake, Garlic, Four Girl, and Firefox on other clowns.

"All the clowns," I screeched, "their faces are Eliminated contestants!"

Poofa said, "I see that. How horrible."

"No kidding!"

"None of those clown-suits complement their masks' skin tones. It's *wrong*."

As soon as Poofa put both feet on the stick of the Corny Dog, the Thrash-clown wrapped his arms around Poofa's waist. Because Poofa and I were gripping each other's forearms, the Thrash-clown failed to pull Poofa off the stick.

But the Thrash-clown *did* manage—

"*Gadzooks*, my pants!"

—to pull Poofa's pants down to his ankles. Every ESPN viewer nationwide saw Poofa's Yellow-Caped Hero briefs.

Too late, I chloroformed the Thrash-clown. Down he went.

With me pulling on Poofa's arm, and Poofa pulling on my arm, and him leaping up with his legs, Poofa and I moved him from the stick up to the pie-shelf of the Corny Dog.

Now all three remaining contestants were atop the Corny Dog.

All the clowns took a step back, and their pie-throwing arms moved to a nonthreatening posture. But the clowns closely and silently watched us three contestants.

I thought, *No more clown-attacks, so that's one less problem I have. Now to pie Cakedough—*

I was just about to turn and face Cakedough when Poofa was jerked away from my side.

****

Cakedough, it turned out, had grabbed Poofa, then had put Poofa in a chokehold.

Cakedough dragged Poofa to the other end of the Corny Dog, far away from the stick. Poofa, both because he was the victim of Cakedough's chokehold, and because his ankles were held together by pulled-down pants, was unable to struggle.

As Cakedough moved to the far end of the Corny Dog, he kicked every pie over the side.

Except for the last pie on the pie-shelf, which clearly he planned to throw at me.

Once Cakedough reached the far end, his left arm stayed wrapped around Poofa's neck in the chokehold. Cakedough's other arm now was holding a pie straight out, but where all Cakedough had to do was to bend his elbow and he would pie Poofa's face.

But during the time that Cakedough had been dragging Poofa and kicking pies, I had reached into my pie-carry bag and had taken out a pie.

By the time Cakedough and Poofa reached the far end of the Corny Dog, I had moved within five feet of the two teen boys, holding a pie in my right hand.

"Let him go!" I said to Cakedough. "You're hurting him!"

Cakedough's voice laughed from inside the fencing mask. "So long as we don't kill Loverboy, our messing with him isn't against any rules."

Meanwhile, the music-box version of "It's A Happy, Happy Day" played from the ice-cream truck's roof speaker.

Clowns silently watched us.

Cakedough said to me, "Here's our brilliant plan: We're going to pie Loverboy. You'll allow this, because we'll stop hurting him as soon as we pie him. Then we'll pie *you*. You'll allow this too. Then we win."

I said, "I don't like that plan."

"No problem, here's Plan B: We throw Loverboy off the Corny Dog. Probably the clowns will pie him, so goodbye Loverboy! Meanwhile, you and us will be throwing pies at each other—except *you* don't have a mask on. So not only will you lose, but Loverboy will be lying on the ground with broken bones. Did we mention that it's five feet from here to the hard ground?"

A man-clown said, "Golly, Miss Twelve Girl has a real problem now."

Meanwhile, Poofa's face was turning redder, as he struggled to both stand upright and to pull Cakedough's hand off his neck. Poofa said something garbled.

"What did he say?" I said to Cakedough. "Let Poofa talk, damn you!"

"Not a problem," the fat boy said. "Let Loverboy say something sweet to his True Love before he gets eliminated."

As Cakedough said this, he moved his arm from Poofa's neck, down to where his hand rested on Poofa's chest. Poofa gasped, and his face quickly regained normal color.

But Poofa said nothing at first.

"*Well?*" Cakedough demanded. "Speak up; we're waiting. And Fire Bitch is waiting too."

Poofa looked at me and mouthed the words *Pie the pie.*

This I did—I flung the pie in my hand to hit the pie in Cakedough's hand.

Cakedough's face showed one second of surprise. In that second, both of Poofa's elbows flew backward, hitting Cakedough in his potbelly. Cakedough fell off the Corny Dog—

Whump! "Ow!"

—landing hard on the ground.

Both my hands were free now. I ran to Poofa and grabbed him before he, too, fell off the Corny Dog.

I murmured, "May I suggest pulling your pants up?"

"How rude," Poofa said, laughing. Then he said, "While I'm getting decent again, find out how Cakedough is doing."

Down on the ground, Cakedough had not yet stood up. A man-clown said to Cakedough, "Gosh, Mr. Two Boy, now it's *you* who has the real problem."

The man-clown yanked the fencing mask off Cakedough's face.

"Hey!" Cakedough yelled. "Leave our mask on! You can't take that off!"

The Firefox-clown said, "Oh? Where in the rules does it say that?"

A man-clown said, "Nothing in the rules against pinning your arms and legs down, either."

Within seconds, four man-clowns had Cakedough pinned to the grass.

The Firefox-clown said, "Poor Mr. Two Boy. You are *helpless* now. Gee whiz, we're going to have *such fun* with you. After we've played with you and played with you, *then* we'll pie you and knock you out. Won't that be fun?"

The Firefox-clown nodded at another woman-clown, who squatted down by Cakedough.

Then Cakedough started to *giggle?*

The squatting woman-clown said, "Kitchy-kitchy-koo. Tickle, tickle, tickle."

"STOP!" Cakedough yelled. "WE'RE TICKLISH, STOP!"

"Tickle, tickle, tickle, *tickle*," the same woman-clown said, as Cakedough went back to giggling.

"HELP US!" Cakedough yelled. "SOMEONE HELP US!"

I thought, *Why let him suffer?* I took out a second pie from my pie-carry bag. While I stood atop the Corny Dog, I threw the pie over and down and—

Splat!

—I hit Cakedough right in the face.

A referee strolled over to Cakedough, glanced down, and said, "He's out. Now we can go home."

****

Seconds later, "Pachelbel's Canon" played. Barnacle Brained announced, "Cakedough Collins of School Zone Two has been eliminated. Two contestants remain."

This was the entire announcement—Poofa's and my Winning was not announced.

Poofa and I walked to the stick-end of the Corny Dog and climbed down. Once we both were on the ground, Poofa rushed to the other end of the Corny Dog and immediately picked up the one pie that remained on the pie-shelf.

I asked, "What do you plan to do with that?" *Is he about to pie me?*

Poofa replied, "I don't trust those clowns, do *you?*"

But even as Poofa said that, the clowns were carrying their unthrown pies to the ice-cream truck, and were handing them back.

When all the clowns' pies were back in the ice-cream truck, two clowns shut the truck's back doors. The ice-cream truck switched its music to "March Of The Toy Soldiers." The ice-cream truck drove away slowly; the clowns formed into parade ranks and marched behind the ice-cream truck.

During all this time, Poofa's and my Winning was not announced.

Poofa said, "Maybe we need to move away from Cakedough, so his golf cart can collect him."

"Worth a try," I said.

Poofa and I walked toward the fake lake. I saw a golf cart roll up to the Corny Dog. After a lot of effort to get limp Cakedough into the golf cart, that golf cart drove away.

Still we heard no announcement about our Winning.

I yelled, "What's the holdup? We won!"

We heard a trumpet fanfare—

Finally!

—followed by Barnacle Brained's voice: "Um, the rule that allowed the last two contestants to be both declared winners if they were from the same school zone, has been revoked. We think the ratings will be better this way. Good luck."

"Aw, *shit*," said a referee. "Make it quick, you two."

****

Poofa was still holding the pie that he had taken from the Corny Dog. I figured he was about to pie me, so I rushed to pull out the one pie that was still in my pie-carry bag.

I was about to throw my pie when Poofa squatted down and set his pie on the grass.

I felt shame for again not trusting Poofa. I squatted down, intending to put my own pie on the ground—

Poofa said, "They have to have a Winner, Karen. Go ahead and pie me, I won't mind."

"*No.*" I finished putting my pie on the ground. "I will *not* pie you, Poofa. *You* pie *me* instead."

"No way," Poofa replied.

A referee commented, "Nuts, another stalemate."

Poofa said, "We both know they have to have a Winner. Please, pie me so Primmy can eat dessert at school."

Then I got a brilliant idea. "What if they *don't* have a Winner?"

Poofa looked confused.

I squatted down again. "Pick up your pie."

****

Seconds later, Poofa and I were standing back to back, each holding a pie in our right hand. My plan was not that Poofa and I would try to pie *each other*, as the Piemakers expected; no, we each were going to pie *ourselves*.

I glanced westward. The sun was setting.

I glanced around at the referees. They were staring at Poofa and me, all wide-eyed.

"On the count of three?" I said.

"On the count of three," Poofa agreed.

"Hold the pie out. I want everyone watching to see what we do."

I whispered, "Take a deep breath, just before."

I called out, "ONE . . . TWO . . ."

I inhaled deeply. I heard Poofa do the same.

"THREE!"

Spla-splat.

A trumpet fanfare began, but Barnacle Brained did not wait for it to finish before he spoke—

"Stop! *Stop!* Ladies and gentlemen, I am pleased to present the Winners of the Pie-Throwing Elimination, Karen Ebergrimm and Poofa Meadowlark! I give you—the contestants of School Zone Twelve!"

Chapter 24
Changing A Lightbulb

With both hands, I grabbed my pie and flung it away from my face. My hands flew back to my face, and I quickly wiped pie-goop off, especially pie-goop that was near my nose and mouth. Only then did I let myself breathe.

I rushed to the shore of the fake lake; Poofa followed close behind me. I dropped to my knees—I got my knees wet, but I did not care—then I used lakewater to clean my face.

When I thought that my face was clean of chloroformed pie-goop, I leaned back and looked around. I saw that Poofa was also kneeling at the water's edge; he was looking at me and grinning.

Poofa said, "You did it, Karen."

I grinned back at him. "No, Poofa, *we* did it."

I shed my dripping-wet, now-empty pie-carry bag. "I guess I don't need this anymore."

****

Soon after that, one golf cart, with two teenagers sharing the passenger seat, brought Poofa and me in front of the school-district stadium's Home bleachers.

It was with great relief that I noted that the Port-A-Potties were gone from outside the cinder-block restrooms.

I had expected the Home seats to be empty—many hours had passed, and the sky was beginning to turn dark. *Empty?* The bleachers were crammed with people—many more than had sat here when the Dessert Games had started.

I was not expecting to see a large crowd of spectators in the twilight. I *certainly* was not expecting them to cheer their lungs out when Poofa and I came into sight.

Poofa was grinning and waving to the crowd. I managed to paste on a smile and make a small, stiff hand-gesture.

The golf cart took us in front of the entire length of the Home bleachers. Then the golf cart continued north, to where the rented tents had been.

Now there were only two tents left; workmen were taking down one of those tents.

Standing in front of the other tent were Sumbitch, Bimbie, Centerd, and Partsane. They all were grinning at Poofa and me.

As soon as I had both feet on the ground, I ran straight to Sumbitch and hugged him.

Sumbitch hugged me back and whispered, "Nice job, dear heart."

Centerd said, "You two are going to love the t-shirts that Partsane and I made."

I said, "Huh? Poofa and I are wearing your t-shirts already."

Centerd said, "Now you're wearing *contestant* t-shirts. We've made special *Winner* t-shirts for you two to wear to the Winner Interview and the Awards Ceremony."

Poofa said, "The Awards Ceremony, I can't wait for that!"

I said, "The Awards Ceremony will *have to* wait. And your new t-shirts, they'll have to wait, too. *I need to pee!*"

I grabbed Bimbie by the wrist, and dragged her to the cinder-block Ladies' Restroom. The two of us got strange looks from the people in the bleachers, but I was past caring.

****

I took two steps into the restroom and stopped dead. I said, "I can't *believe* this."

Bimbie also had stopped walking. "You men should *not* be here."

In front of us were the three men from HFH Repairs. The man with the funny haircut was at the top of a stepladder, holding a lightbulb up against a light fixture in the ceiling. The man with the curly hair and the bald-headed man were *turning* the stepladder that the first man was standing on.

The two men turned the ladder half a turn before they set the ladder down—all while huffing and puffing.

"Sorry, ladies," said the man with the funny haircut, "but Mr. Ice said we can't leave till we get this lightbulb in. We're going as fast as we can, but it's taking too long."

The curly-haired man said, "It's taking too long because he's gotten *fat*."

The bald-headed man said, "I'll say."

The man with the funny haircut hit each of the other two men on top of the head with a fist. "No, it's taking too long because you two are *weaklings*. You're holding up these ladies, you knuckleheads! Let's go, let's go!"

The two worker-men picked up the stepladder again, but managed only a third of a turn before they set the ladder down. Again they were panting.

I said, "Guys, I *really* need you out of here *soon*. Can I help with that?"

The man with the funny haircut looked me up and down. "No offense, lady, but you don't look strong."

Bimbie said, "I'll have you know that Karen here just won the Dessert Games! She's brave and smart."

The bald-headed man said, "I like brave dames! This doesn't mean you're strong, though."

Bimbie said, "Karen is smart. She's an *inventor!* I'm hoping she'll invent a machine to turn coal into pearls."

I said to the three men, "Look, here's what we do. You, come down off the stepladder."

As soon as the man with the funny haircut was off the stepladder, I climbed up it.

As soon as my hand touched the lightbulb, the funny-haircut man grabbed part of the stepladder and said to the other two, "Now lift."

I said, "*No!* Stop! Put the ladder down—"

"Then how are you gonna screw in the lightbulb?" Funny-Haircut Man asked.

"I'll show you. All three of you, step back and watch me."

Seconds later, all three men were looking up at me with puzzled expressions.

I said, "You don't need to turn the ladder, you need only turn your hand. Like so."

I demonstrated, using my right hand. Seconds later, the lightbulb was screwed in tight and the lightbulb was glowing.

As I was climbing down the stepladder, the bald-headed man said, "She's a *smart* dame too."

The curly-haired man said, "For sure, smarter than *him*."

The man with the funny haircut said, "Shaddap, you two!" He poked his helpers in their eyes. *Boink.*

I was just about to flood the entire bathroom. With fists clenched (and another muscle clenched), I yelled, "GUYS, TAKE IT OUTSIDE!"

The three men and their stepladder were gone quickly. I got myself to a bathroom stall barely in time.

****

As soon as I walked out of the bathroom stall, Bimbie said, "You have to hurry. We're keeping Superintendent Ice and everyone else waiting."

Some things never change.

Soon afterward (but not soon enough to please Bimbie), I was back in the School Zone Twelve stylists' tent.

I was surprised to see Poofa, both for what he was wearing, and for what he was *not* wearing.

Poofa was wearing a black t-shirt that had *Panem ISD Pie-Throwing Elimination* and *SZ 12* silk-screened on the front in white. Below the *SZ 12* were silk-screened letters of yellow, orange, and red; the letters looked like flames. The flame-letters spelled out *Winner: EberLark.*

What Poofa was *not* wearing was makeup. I was shocked.

Poofa must have read my mind; he said, "I told Partsane no. Told her, Put nothing on my face."

Centerd said, "I hope you like Poofa's shirt, Karen, because I made one just like it for *you.*"

A minute later, I was wearing Centerd's new t-shirt. The way it fit me was wondrous, and I liked how Poofa smiled when he saw me wearing it.

Bimbie said, "Now that we're all dressed in our new clothes, we need to go to the Winner Interview and Awards Ceremony *now.* Superintendent Ice is *waiting.* And Mr. Flickactor too, the poor man."

"Hold on a second," Centerd said. He pinned the gold dancing-hippo pin onto my brand-new t-shirt.

****

A man walked in; he was wearing Panem ISD overalls and carrying a toolbox. "I'm here to take off two ankle-trackers."

"Later," Bimbie snapped. "Right now, we're keeping *important* people waiting."

"Then the important people can wait *longer*," I said to Bimbie.

I said to the technician, "Do Poofa's first, then mine. I can't tell you what a relief it will be to be *free* of this thing."

I did not have any money to tip the technician with, so I tipped him two bottles of chloroform.

Chapter 25
Oh Primmy, Primmy!

Minutes later, Poofa and I were sitting on stage with Sid Caesar Flickactor. But before Sid interviewed us, Poofa and I got the "privilege" of watching a very special video on the giant TV.

First the TV screen showed a stern FBI notice, "Piracy Is Worse Than Kidnapping, Rape, And Murder Combined." Then we had to sit through seventeen promos for other sporting events that ESPN would cover soon. At last, the TV showed the Corny Dog and twenty-four teenagers ringed around it.

I got to see what the audience had seen: how Poofa had flimflammed the Gluttons with "I offered her my heart, but she turned me down cold, so now I want to be with you when she gets pieed." Poofa's scheme had been working great, right up to the moment I had showed up in my fake-referee outfit and had tried pieing Gluttons.

Right after Poofa had told me, "Karen, get out of here! Get going! I'll hold him off," Cakedough had punched him, *hard*, in the jewels.

Now sitting next to me, Poofa sucked in his breath. He murmured to me, "Even watching it on TV, it's painful."

****

Minutes later, Sid was smiling at Poofa and me. "Karen, we all want to know: When did you fall in love with Poofa?"

I was not expecting this question. "Gosh, that is a really hard—I mean, it all depends on what—"

Sid looked at the audience. "I know when *I* knew you loved him. When they announced the two-contestants, same-school-zone rule, then you yelled Poofa's name."

The audience *aww*ed—except for one male voice that yelled, "Yeah!"

Poofa smiled at me. "You really did that? Thank you."

I thought, *I have to say this, even if everyone hates me for it.* "Actually, Mr. Flickactor, I don't *love* Poofa. Not like he *loves* me—"

Now the audience's *aww* sounded distressed.

"—but I *like* him. A lot."

The audience applauded. Poofa looked relieved.

Sid asked, "And when did you know you *liked* him?"

"When I discovered that Poofa was wearing Yellow-Caped Hero briefs in the hot tub, but I still kissed him."

"Can we show a clip?" Sid asked.

They could. The clip showed Poofa from the back, right after the Thrash-clown had de-pantsed him. Poofa's butt, and the Yellow-Caped Hero underwear that covered his butt, both were clearly visible.

Now Poofa covered his eyes with his hand. He muttered, "First Cakedough punching me in the nuts, now *this*."

I studied the clip and I said, "Lifting hundred-pound sacks of flour has been good for you."

The audience laughed. I had no clue why.

Sid asked me next, "Karen, the moment when you suggested you each pie yourself—what was going through your mind, hm?"

Again his question caught me unprepared. I said, "I don't know, I just . . . couldn't bear the thought of . . . Ice letting me eat dessert in the cafeteria but Poofa couldn't."

Again the audience *aww*ed. Poofa squeezed my hand.

By now, Superintendent Ice was standing by the stage, holding two blue boxes. Ice was glaring at me.

****

Superintendent Ice was wearing white gloves when he presented a blue box to Poofa and me each. Ice's voice and posture both were ceremonial.

The boxes were covered with blue silk. They weren't tall at all, but they were wide enough, and long enough, to each hold a sheet of letter-sized paper.

I opened my box. Inside was one piece of paper, titled "DESSERT PRIVILEGE." As expected, there were blank lines for Transferee's Name, Transferee's School, and Transferee's School Zone, where I could sign Dessert Privilege over to Primmy. The lines for Winner's Name, Winner's School, and Winner's School Zone were filled in, with correct information about me. My signature-line was blank. Superintendent Ice's signature-line already bore his signature—

—along with a handwritten addition, "Dessert Privilege is for even-numbered days of the month *only*."

I looked over at the paper that Poofa was holding. *His* Dessert Privilege was for odd-numbered days.

My eyes went to the face of Verylongnameus Ice. He was smiling a cruel smile. "Miss Ebergrimm, you never were *both* promised the *entire* prize."

Ice's hand reached forward, to pull my braid off my shoulder. I looked down; the gold dancing-hippo pin gleamed in the stage lights.

"What a lovely pin," Ice said. His words were polite, but his tone of voice was angry.

I smiled and replied, "Thank you. I picked it up off the ground, but it's brought me luck."

Ice said, "May your luck continue."

****

The only "official" transportation back to PHS Twelve for Sumbitch, Poofa, and me was that slowpoke Studebaker bus. But Bimbie offered to drive us home in her car.

Bimbie talked during the entire drive.

Sumbitch drank from a hip flask during the entire drive.

Poofa tried to catch my eye during the entire drive.

Sometimes I looked at Poofa and smiled at him. Sometimes I looked away.

Once Bimbie's car entered School Zone Twelve, Bimbie asked Poofa and me where we lived. She did not, I noticed, ask Sumbitch where *he* lived.

The simple topic of *Whom do I drop off first?* flustered Bimbie for some reason. Or rather, she was flustered till Sumbitch said, "Drop me off first, Queenie, but walk me to the door. Give the kids a moment of privacy."

Minutes later, Bimbie's car was pulled up in front of Sumbitch's house. I was shocked to discover that Sumbitch was not only not homeless, but his house was *huge*.

Sumbitch grinned at me. "Surprised, dear heart? After I won the Pie-Throwing Elimination, I decided I liked winning things. I went from zero to ambitious in one day."

But one thing stopped Sumbitch's house from being called a *mansion*: It had a geese pen in back. Even from the curb in front of his house, I could hear those geese.

Bimbie said, "They're *rude*. They always honk early in the morning." Then she gasped, realizing what she had said.

As requested, Bimbie walked Sumbitch to his front door. She claimed she was doing it because he was drunk.

****

Bimbie and Sumbitch had left Bimbie's car. Poofa and I were alone.

I broke the silence: "You know, I like you better, Poofa, without all that makeup."

Poofa replied, "Well, I like *you* better *romantic*."

****

As soon as Bimbie got back in her car, Poofa asked her, "Do you have a pen and paper I can borrow, please?"

Bimbie said, "How delightful! Karen wants to give you her phone number!"

"Something like that," Poofa said, as I blushed. "Bimbie, could you turn on the overhead light, please?" By now it was full dark outside.

Then, in the back seat where Bimbie could not see, Poofa wrote out and gave me his phone number. I stuck the paper in the pocket of my jeans.

But I did not promise then to call him, nor did I make any such promise when I got out of Bimbie's car.

I did not kiss Poofa goodbye when I got out of Bimbie's car, though clearly he wished I would.

My last sight of Poofa that day was of him looking at me through the car window, as Bimbie's car drove away. Poofa was looking at me with a hopeful expression.

****

I had given Primmy my purse, back when today's adventure had started. So not only had I been unable to phone or to text Primmy all day, but now I had to ring the doorbell in order to enter my house.

Time passed after I rang the doorbell before Primmy opened the door. Her arm and leg in a cast slowed her down.

I said, "Guess what, I won! Well, I *half*-won—"

Now Primmy was squeezing me. "Karen, I'm *so* glad you're home! This day has been awful!"

"*Awful?* What happened? Tell me!"

"Sally was over here. I invited her over because I thought she needed a nice friend. No nice girls are friends with Sally, right? Anyway, Sally got here, then she asked if she could invite some of her not-nice friends over. I didn't want to, but I said yes. Soon they were all here, eating our food and drinking Dad's beer out in the garage. But I didn't say anything because I thought Sally needed a nice friend, right? Then the mail came, and I got a package in the mail—"

"*You* got a package in the mail?" I said. Soozin had ordered something for *me* from Acme Novelty, and he had promised that it would come today.

"So I opened up the box, and it was some kind of seat cushion. Which confused me, because only grandmothers use seat cushions and I'm not a grandmother."

I was getting a bad feeling where this story was headed.

Primmy continued, "Then Joanna—she's a friend of Sally's with a super-trashy mouth—whispered something to the others. They giggled, including Sally, but nobody told me the secret. Then Sally asked me, 'Do you know what this is?' I said, 'It's a seat cushion for old ladies.' Then Joanna grabbed it out of the box, walked over to the dining-room chair where Dad used to sit, pulled the chair out, put the cushion on the chair, and said, 'It's a *special* cushion. *Sit.*' "

Now I was alarmed. I had heard stories about Joanna— the most famous story being where Joanna, a boy, and his girlfriend had been in an elevator. Joanna had stripped naked, just because she had not liked the girlfriend. In another story, Joanna had stuck a girl in the arm with a knife while they were working together. Joanna was *crazy*.

Primmy continued, "I didn't like being bossed around in my own house, but I let it slide. I walked over to Dad's chair—

202 *Tom H. Richardson*

and all these girls started *giggling*. Then I sat down. Oh *god*, Karen, it was *awful*, what happened next!"

"You sat on the cushion, and it made a farty noise."

Primmy nodded. "It made a *loud* farty noise. *Loud*, like when you step on Pollen's tail and he yowls. Anyway, all the girls started laughing at me, and Joanna called me 'stupid.' Then all the other girls started chanting, 'Stupid Primmy, stupid Primmy,' including Sally. They made me *cry*, and I was dying of embarrassment."

I hugged my little sister.

"So I told Sally and them to get the *fuck* out of my house."

****

The cushion was still on Dad's chair. I sat on it—and sure enough, the farty noise was loud. Primmy cringed.

Seconds later, I was examining the cushion. On the outside of the cushion was a cloth cover, which had a zipper to open it with.

Inside the cover, as I had expected, was a self-inflating whoopee cushion. Also inside was Soozin's addition: a chip-card that was inside a clear plastic envelope. Attached to the chip-card was a transistor-radio battery, a cheap and simple microphone, and a small speaker. Dental floss tied the microphone to the sound-tube of the whoopee cushion.

But why did Primmy think the box was for her, not me? Aloud, I said, "Primmy, bring me the box this came in."

Today's rain had blurred the shipping label; I could not read parts of the address. I could not read *Ebergrimm*, and I could not tell whether the letter before the last name was a *K* or a *P*. Neither could Primmy, it seemed.

****

"Hey, Karen," Soozin said when I called him. His voice sounded wary. "I saw you on ESPN today."

"Actually, I'm calling about the box that came to my house today."

Soozin sounded proud: "My 'new and improved' whoopee cushion? What did you think when you sat on it?"

"Actually, it was *Primmy* who sat on it. You made her die of embarrassment, Soozin Hawtbod."

I then gave Soozin a summary of what had happened with Primmy and the whoopee cushion.

Soozin said, "I didn't intend for any of this to happen."

"I believe you. Still, you invented it, and your invention made Primmy die of embarrassment. Which means you and I are *done*, forever, except as friends."

"We can't ever *date?* You're *friendzoning* me?"

"Yes. Because your invention made Primmy die of embarrassment."

"*Fine*. Have fun with your *baker*." Soozin ended the call.

****

A few minutes later, I was telling Primmy about my day's adventures when my smartphone rang. I did not recognize the phone number.

Calling was Midget Underwater. She said, "You have my gold dancing-hippo pin. And you wore it on television!"

"I'll text you my address and you can come get your pin tomorrow," I said. "Now if you'll excuse me—"

Midget's voice was gleeful: "Soozin just called me up and asked me for a date. And I have *you* to thank. *Really*, Karen, you put *Soozin Hawtbod* in the Friend Zone?"

****

After I talked to Primmy, I called up Poofa's phone number. I told him, "Long story short: I won't be dating Soozin. Do you still want to go out with me?"

"Wow! Sure I do. Tomorrow is Sunday, right? You want to have a date tomorrow afternoon? Wait, hold on, I'm sure Mom won't let me borrow the car."

I said, "But you have a bike, right? How about tomorrow afternoon we have a picnic in my back yard?"

"That'll work. I'll bring over meats, cheeses, and bread. You like cheese buns? And I'll bring a toaster."

I blinked. "A *toaster?*"

"You're the only girl I want to toast bread with, Karen. But I'll try not to burn the toast; you wouldn't like that."

"Yeah, if you burned the bread, this would kill our relationship forever."

Poofa laughed, then his voice got serious: "Karen, are you *sure* you want to go out with me?"

"Yes, Poofa. I'm sure because you're kind and gentle, and because I've seen you with your shirt off."

"That last one confuses me."

"You have no idea, the effect you can have."

THE END